'It's leap year, Raul. Will you marry me?'

'Now I get it,' he laughed mirthlessly. 'The arguments of the last few weeks, the defiance, and then the grand finale—staying out all night. What kind of fool do you take me for, Penny? Better women than you have tried to manipulate me into marriage and failed. You're good, but not that good.'

His comment was like a knife in her heart. 'I take it that was a no,' she got out between clenched teeth.

'Correct, honey. If and when I take a wife, I will do the asking.'

Jacqueline Baird began writing as a hobby when her family objected to the smell of her oil painting, and immediately became hooked on the romantic genre. She loves travelling and worked her way around the world from Europe to the Americas and Australia, returning to marry her teenage sweetheart. She lives in Ponteland, Northumbria, the county of her birth, and has two teenage sons. She enjoys playing badminton, and spends most weekends with husband Jim, sailing their Gp.14 around Derwent Reservoir.

Recent titles by the same author:

A DEVIOUS DESIRE
THE VALENTINE CHILD

RAUL'S REVENGE

BY
JACQUELINE BAIRD

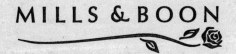

MILLS & BOON

MILLS & BOON and the Rose Device
are trademarks of the publisher.
Harlequin Mills & Boon Limited,
Eton House, 18-24 Paradise Road, Richmond, Surrey TW9 1SR

© Jacqueline Baird 1996

ISBN 0 263 79553 5

Set in Times Roman 10 on 12 pt.
01-9607-57360 C1

Made and printed in Great Britain

CHAPTER ONE

'NICE bed, Raul.' Penny glanced at the huge bed in the centre of the hotel room, then, blonde head tilting to one side, shot a sexy, sidelong glance at her companion. 'And we did miss siesta!'

'Wanton.' Raul grinned, and, dropping the case on the bed, added, 'Sorry, no time. You unpack while I shower. A car is picking me up in thirty minutes.'

Penny followed the tall dark man's progress towards the *en suite* bathroom with wistful eyes. Business always came first with Raul. Sighing, she did as he had suggested and unpacked the clothes, then, kicking off her sandals, flopped down on the bed and gazed around yet another hotel bedroom. At one time she would have been delighted by the luxury, now she found one hotel room much like another.

She heard the sound of water running in the bathroom and a deep bass voice belting out, singing off key in Spanish. A soft smile curved her lips. Raul, true to form, was performing his usual lusty caterwauling in the shower. The noise stopped and Penny swung her legs to the floor. Sitting up, she brushed her long hair tidily behind her ears, her blue eyes eager with anticipation.

It was stupid, she knew. She had lived with the man for months, she loved him more than life, but he just had to enter a room and she was breathless. A moment later the bathroom door opened and Raul strolled out.

She knew every inch of his magnificent body as well as she knew her own, but the sight of him never failed

5

to make her pulse race and her stomach clench with excitement. He wasn't a particularly handsome man—his nose was too large and his chin too square—but thick night-black hair and unusual gold-flecked deep brown eyes combined with six feet three inches and two hundred pounds of hard-packed muscle added up to a powerful specimen of the male sex.

At the moment his only covering was a white towel slung low around his lean hips, and as he prowled around the room, flinging open doors and drawers to find his clothes, Penny's eyes lingered lovingly on his bronzed torso and the thick mat of black curls covering his chest, arrowing down to disappear beneath the towel. As she watched he raised a long-fingered hand to scratch idly the downy covering on his muscular chest.

'*Dios*! I'm going to be late,' Raul grumbled, turning towards the bed. A pair of black silk boxer shorts dangling in one large hand, he flashed her a brilliant glance. 'So don't even think of persuading me into bed.'

'Me persuade you!' Penny's blue eyes lit with amusement. 'As if I would!' she exclaimed, all fake innocence.

His wide mouth curved in a sensuous smile. 'You, anywhere near a bed, Penny, could provoke a dying octogenarian.'

'You're not that old,' she mocked.

'Brat.' And, sitting down beside her, he caught her hand in his, and with his other hand he pushed the stray tendrils of fine blonde hair from her brow, his expression suddenly serious.

'I am sorry about this.' He glanced around the room and back to her face. 'I know I promised you we would be in London for your birthday.' With a Latin shrug of his shoulders, he added, 'But these things happen.'

'It's all right, Raul,' Penny reassured him. 'How many girls can arrive at a Spanish airport expecting to go to London and end up in the Middle East for the night?' She tried to make light of the upset to their plans. 'Unless, of course, you've added white slaving to your business empire?' she teased.

'Don't even joke about it.' Raul grimaced. 'Not in this country; you're mine, and mine you will stay, so don't you forget it.'

'Yes, oh master...' She bowed her head in mock subservience while her small hand teasingly stroked his muscular thigh. Her action was greeted with a guffaw of laughter.

'Witch...behave yourself; I really do have to leave you for a few hours, but I'll make it up to you later, and that's a promise.'

They had left Raul's home that morning to catch a plane for London. A call on his car phone had resulted in his having to attend an emergency meeting in Dubai. Luckily there had been a scheduled flight to the Middle East some ten minutes after the London flight. Before Penny had known what was happening she had found herself in the first-class section of a Boeing 747 heading across the Mediterranean.

Penny had become used to Raul flying off around the world at a moment's notice. As the owner of a large international engineering company, along with a *hacienda* and a few thousand acres in the Andalusian area of Spain, plus a host of other interests, her boyfriend was an extremely wealthy man.

Her lips twitched in the briefest of wry smiles. 'Boyfriend' was hardly the right word, she admitted to herself, her deep blue eyes searching his hard face. At thirty-seven Raul Da Silva couldn't be called a boy by anyone...

'That's what I like about you, Penny, darling—you
never fuss,' Raul offered complacently, rising from the
bed after first driving her almost senseless with a long,
hard kiss.

Fighting to recover her breath, Penny watched as he
moved around the room, all male efficiency, and marvelled at how easily he switched from passionate lover
to hard-nosed business tycoon. Exactly three minutes
later he stood beside the bed, elegantly dressed in a grey,
three-piece silk suit, the white of his shirt contrasting
with the dark bronze of his rugged features, a blue and
grey striped tie at his strong throat. He stuck out his
arm.

'Fasten these cuff-links for me, honey.' She did,
smiling slightly at the 'honey'. Raul spoke perfect English
but with an endearing trace of an American accent.

'Thanks, Penny; I don't know what I would do
without you.' He smiled down at her, his golden eyes
glowing, and like a magician presenting a rabbit from a
hat he slid his hand into his jacket pocket and withdrew
a square velvet box. 'I was going to give you this over
a candlelit dinner at your favourite restaurant by the
Thames, but under the circumstances you'd better have
it now. Something for you to gloat over while I'm gone.'

Penny's lashes lowered to hide the sudden disappointment in her eyes. She had been hoping against hope
that her birthday present would be a ring, but one glance
at the box and she knew how wrong she was. Hiding her
disappointment behind a bright smile, she took the box
from Raul's outstretched hand and opened it.

A gasp of amazement escaped her. Inside was an exquisite diamond bracelet fit for a queen.

'Happy birthday, darling. Do you like it?'

'What's not to like? It is magnificent. Thank you,' she said softly, and, holding it out to him, murmured, 'Put it on for me.' She kept her head bent as he fastened the exquisite jewels around her wrist, supposedly admiring it. 'It must have cost you a fortune; you're spoiling me.' She tried to smile but she could not look at him in case he saw the moisture glazing her eyes.

A long finger tilted her chin up. 'That's another of the things I adore about you, Penny; you're such an emotional little thing and you're not afraid to show it.' And with his other hand he wiped the solitary tear from her cheek. 'Hey, you deserve it, darling—you're so good for me.'

But was he good for her? Penny wondered, and then hated herself for the disloyal thought, simply because he had given her a bracelet when she longed for a ring and had completely misread the cause of her tears. Raul was not an insensitive man, he simply saw only what suited himself and his high-powered, workaholic lifestyle.

She glanced at him as his hand fell from her face, and abruptly he straightened up. But he was not looking at her. He had already left, if not in body then certainly in spirit. She knew the signs.

A frown marring his broad brow, he checked the flat gold Rolex on his wrist. 'I have to go. You rest, and if I'm not back by eight this evening order dinner in the suite,' he commanded briskly. Turning, he strode across the room and, with a careless backward wave of his hand and a casual 'see you later' he left, Penny forgotten and his whole attention on the meeting ahead.

Rest. She didn't feel like resting. She stood up, the glitter of diamonds on her wrist catching her eye, and with a soft sigh she removed the bracelet from her arm and dropped it on the bedside table before walking into the bathroom.

The scent of Raul hung in the air and she breathed in greedily as she discarded her clothes. She loved Raul and she was sure that he loved her, even if he never said so in as many words. He showed it in a hundred ways. He was unfailingly generous—as a man and, more importantly, as a lover—he looked after her every need, he protected her. And also himself, a devilish imp of mischief echoed in her brain. He never forgot birth control; he was taking no chances on being trapped into marriage, that was for sure.

Penny shook her head to dispel the unsettling thought. She was ungrateful, she told herself firmly. Simply because he had given her a bracelet worth a fortune rather than the ring she had secretly hoped for.

She was about to step into the shower, and then changed her mind. Instead she picked up a bottle of bath oil and, tipping half of it into the tub, leant over the huge white marble bath and turned on the taps. Why not luxuriate in a scented tub for a change? She certainly had the time...

God! What was the matter with her today? She wasn't usually restless, and it was so childish to be upset over a damned birthday.

Straightening to her full height of five feet five inches, she surveyed herself in the mirrored wall of the bathroom. Months spent mostly in a warm climate had streaked her long ash-blonde hair almost white in places. Usually she wore it in a twist or braid but today, at Raul's insistence, she had worn it loose, simply brushed behind her ears and falling in soft waves down past her shoulder blades. Her breasts were high and firm, with a few rosy marks left by Raul last night. Her waist was narrow, her stomach flat and her hips gently curved. Her legs were long in comparison to her height, and well shaped.

Running her hands through her hair, she lifted it up in a bunch, revealing the long line of her throat, the firm chin. She had a wide, generous mouth—maybe a bit too wide—a small, straight nose, and large deep blue eyes.

Her skin glowed with health and a light golden tan; she was not one for sunbathing excessively—she was too fair in any case. But all in all she was not bad for twenty-two— No, twenty-three, she reminded herself, as of today, and with determined cheerfulness she turned off the taps and stepped into the tub.

She sank down beneath the soothing water and laid her head back, closed her eyes and willed her mind to go blank—something she was becoming remarkably adept at doing. But that wasn't so surprising because, while at college studying pharmacy, she had also taken a course in yoga to help her to relax. Whether one was supposed to use the technique in the bath, she didn't really know, and didn't much care as long as it worked.

Half an hour later she opened her eyes, the rapidly cooling water making her shiver. Quickly she stepped out of the bath and into the shower. Minutes later, with her long hair freshly washed, she took a towel from the towel-rail and wrapped it around her head. She reached out for a larger one and, unfolding it, read the name embossed in the thick, fluffy fabric: Hyatt Regency. So that was where they were staying.

Penny paused in the process of wrapping the towel around her naked body, and slowly shook her head. There was something terribly depressing, she realised sadly, about being reduced to reading the hotel towels to remind herself where she was... How and when had the thrill of foreign travel and luxury hotels faded into simply waiting for Raul?

She didn't try to answer the question—she didn't dare—and in a flurry of activity she dried her hair, brushing it until it hung like a soft curtain of silk over her shoulders.

She lingered over applying her make-up, but as she only used a moisturiser and a touch of eyeshadow and mascara, the finishing touch being a natural lip-gloss, she was ready by seven. She slipped into a straight, halter-necked dress of soft ivory crêpe—deceptively simple but cunningly cut to curve around her breasts without needing a bra, and leaving her back bare, with the skirt ending just over her knees.

Raul had objected to her wearing miniskirts, which, considering they were popular these days, was endearingly old-fashioned of him. Or was it? she found herself questioning again, and shook her head irritably. Apart from her shoes, she was ready.

Idly she strolled into the sitting room of the suite and, crossing to the French doors, flung them back and stepped onto the balcony. After the air-conditioned comfort of indoors the heat hit her like a blowtorch, but the view took her breath away.

This was her first visit to an Arab country, and the landscape was alien but magnificent. Dubai lay before her, sparkling white, pristine clean, with towering buildings, fantastically delicate minarets and, in the distance, the blue of the Gulf.

After drinking in the sight, she walked back into the room and picked up the information provided by the hotel. Dropping into a comfortable, soft leather chair, she read with interest of the restaurants and bars of the shopping arcade incorporated in the building. Better yet, situated close to the city centre as the hotel was, it was only five minutes' walk to the gold souk...

Eight o'clock came, but Raul didn't. Penny, with a determined glint in her blue eyes, picked up her small ivory clutch bag, slipped her feet in matching fabric strappy sandals and without a second thought walked out of the room and across the corridor into the elevator.

It was her birthday, and, by heaven, she was going to enjoy it. Not for her a meal in the room; a snack in one of the restaurants and a stroll around the gold souk sounded much more fun.

After a light meal, and armed with a small diagram from the hotel receptionist, Penny walked out into the cooler night air and turned left as instructed.

She had only walked two paces when she heard a car door slam and a voice snap, 'Penelope.' A firm hand closed around her upper arm and swung her around. 'Where the hell do you think you're going?' was hissed in her ear as she gazed up in surprise at Raul's taut features.

'Raul, you're back. I was—'

'Shut up,' he grated, and it was then that she saw his two companions alight from the long white stretch limousine—one a gentleman in a Western-style suit, and the other a man taller even than Raul and draped in the flowing white robes of an Arab sheikh.

'Raul, you must introduce me to this charming creature,' the Arab commanded.

'Of course, your highness; allow me to present...' Raul hesitated '...my companion, Miss Penelope Gold.' And, looking down at Penny, his dark eyes cold as ice, he continued, 'Penny, this is Sheikh Ali Ben Hammat.'

For the first time in their relationship Penny felt truly embarrassed, and coldly furious at being introduced as a *companion*. Good manners alone brought a polite smile to her wide mouth, while there was no mistaking the blatant, sensual interest in the Sheikh's black eyes as he caught her hand and raised it to his lips.

'Charmed,' he murmured. 'I'm honoured to meet such an exquisitely lovely young lady.' And, reluctantly releasing her hand, he added, 'Señor Da Silva is an extremely lucky man.'

'Thank you,' she mumbled, but it took all her self-control not to cry out—not because of the kiss but because Raul's fingers on her arm tightened to such a degree that she thought he would draw blood.

The conversation that ensued was lost on Penny, simply because the men spoke in Arabic. But ten minutes later she found out...

The walk through the hotel and the ride up in the elevator had been conducted in a tense, angry silence, and now, as the door swung closed behind Raul and he finally let go of her arm, Penny swung around, her blue eyes flashing fury. But, before she could open her mouth and demand an explanation for his ill-mannered, overbearing conduct, Raul silenced her with a string of curses that made the colour surge in her face.

He had never spoken that way in front of her before. But then, as her blue eyes clashed with furious black, she realised that she had never seen him so angry before. Involuntarily she took a step back; she could see the barely leashed tension in every line of his tall body, and felt suddenly threatened by it.

'What the hell did you think you were doing?' he snapped. 'Have you gone stark, raving mad?'

Penny shrank back from the black rage in his eyes, but before she could answer his wild accusations he added furiously, 'Look at you—a dress that reveals every curve... My God! Do you have to flirt with every man you meet, and in Dubai?' Suddenly he caught her shoulders, his long fingers biting into her flesh. Her head fell back and she was looking up into his bitterly twisted features. 'A sheikh no less...'

'I don't know what you're talking about... I wasn't flirting with anyone. I was going for a walk—'

'A walk—on your own—in a Arab country—at night.'

She flinched as he shot the words at her like the staccato fire of a machine gun, only inches from her pale face.

'You have good reason to cringe. Their own women aren't even allowed out without being draped from head to foot in black. A white woman on her own is considered little better than a whore and fair game.' His hard mouth twisted in a sneer. 'You had to know that, Penny. Even you are not that dumb.'

She gasped in outrage. Dumb was she? 'If anyone is dumb around here it's you,' she shot back. 'Dragging me through the hotel and back here like a sack of potatoes. Frothing at the mouth because I smiled at a man *you* introduced me too.'

'Smiled? Simpered, more like. Have you any idea what you have done? You almost cost me a multi-million-dollar deal for the desalination plant.'

'You're crazy. The heat has got to you.' Penny shook her head, unable to associate this glowering stranger with the man she had lived with for the past few months.

'Your heat certainly got the Sheikh,' Raul sneered cynically. 'I have just spent the worst five minutes of my life trying to explain in not very good Arabic why I could not sell him my companion. You, Penny! He wanted you as one of his concubines...'

His mouth twisted in a bitter parody of a smile. 'Luckily he did offer to wait until I was finished with you. But I still had the devil's own job talking him out of it, and now I'm going to have to stay here a lot longer to oversee the alterations, simply so as not to offend the man further.'

Feeling like kicking him, she tore herself out of his hold and shot across the room, tears stinging her eyes. She was furious and so hurt... Now she knew what he really thought of her.

Spinning on her heel, she looked back at him. He was standing, all outraged masculine aggression. Her blue eyes ran over his tall, fit body. She loved him, but the Sheikh was obviously an astute man. He had seen what Penny had refused to acknowledge...

'Perhaps if you had not hesitated over introducing me as your *companion*—' she drawled the word scathingly '—he would not have considered me concubine material in the first place. The Sheikh is a man of the world, with a good grasp of English. Companion. Concubine. Where is the difference?' she demanded bitterly, and almost laughed at the look of outrage on Raul's dark face.

'Is that what you truly think? Is that how you truly imagine I see our relationship?' Raul asked, slightly incredulous, but with an icy authority that demanded an answer.

She stared back at him. 'I think—' She stopped. She didn't know what she thought any more.

When she had first met Raul it had all seemed so perfect—like fate, destiny. She had been working the late shift in the Kensington branch of a national drugs company that had employed her as a pharmacist.

It had been a black, blustery night at the end of January when Raul had dashed into the shop with a prescription which he'd said was for his housekeeper Mrs Grimble's angina. The old lady had forgotten to have it filled and he had not liked the idea of her being without her medication. Penny had thought what a caring man he was and her admiration had risen another notch when he'd declared that it was very dangerous for a lovely young girl like herself to be alone in a pharmacy at night.

They had got talking and Penny had remarked on his slight accent. He'd told her that he was Spanish and she remembered her response with a sad smile.

'But you're too tall to be Spanish.'

Raul had laughed out loud and gently mocked her. 'A commonly held prejudice of northern Europeans, but may I point out Prince Felipe of Spain is well in excess of six feet? Your Prince Charles is around five-nine, no?'

Admitting her mistake, they had laughed together. But she had sensibly refused his offer to come back at closing time, to give her a lift home. The company had provided taxis for the late staff. But the following afternoon Raul had appeared again and persuaded her to have dinner with him.

That had been the start of their relationship. For the next two months, whenever he'd been in London, he'd called her, wined and dined her, taken her to the theatre, the opera, and opened up a world of wealth and sophistication that she had never thought to aspire to, and finally he had taken her to his bed.

How naïve she had been! Penny thought, closing her eyes for an instant as the memory washed over her. Raul had made love to her with all the tender passion and expertise he possessed. Her passage from virgin to woman had been a revelation, a feast of the senses, an explosion of emotions that she had never imagined possible.

It had been the most perfect night of her life, and, the morning after, lying curled up against the hard heat of his male body, she had foolishly asked when they were getting married.

Raul had quickly dismissed the suggestion, declaring that because he was so much older, more experienced than she it would not be fair to rush her into marriage. She might change her mind. Most girls after their first time confused love with sex.

Instead he had suggested that she give up her job and move in with him. He had made it all sound very sensible, as if he was doing her a favour.

She shook her head, her pale hair floating around her shoulders, an unfamiliar cynical smile curving her lovely mouth. Ripe for the plucking, sprang to mind.

'You bitch.'

Her head shot back, Raul's snarling comment shocking her out of her reverie. His dark eyes glittered with rage and in one lithe stride he was in front of her, his strong hands grasping her shoulders. 'I—' she began.

'Don't bother to lie; your silence is answer enough,' he growled, just before his mouth crashed down on hers in a brutal parody of a lover's kiss.

Penny lifted her hands to the hard wall of his chest, trying to push him away. But he was too big, too strong, and, sensing her resistance, he swept one arm around her tiny waist, hauling her off her feet, while his other hand twisted the length of her hair around his fingers, pulling her face back, the better to ravish her mouth.

'No, Raul,' she gasped as his mouth left hers to savage her throat with hot, burning kisses.

He raised his head, his black eyes implacable in their intent. 'No? You dare to say no?' he grated harshly. 'You have a lot to learn for a woman who thinks she is a concubine. They are not allowed to say no.'

Penny began to struggle in earnest, kicking out wildly with her feet, her small hands pushing at his massive shoulders, but with no effect. Raul simply hoisted her over his shoulder and stalked into the bedroom while she pummelled his back with her clenched fists in vain.

'Put me down, you great, hulking brute!' she screamed. She would not allow him to treat her like this, she vowed.

Suddenly she was falling backwards onto the bed, all the breath leaving her body with the force of the impact. She gazed up at the man standing over her. It was a Raul she had never seen before. He was out of control, his lips pulled back in the travesty of a smile, his dark eyes flashing fire.

His hand reached down and tore the halter-neck of her dress to her waist, revealing her braless state. She put her hands to cover herself and he tore them away, spreading them either side of her head as he bent to kneel over her, straddling her lower body with his long legs.

His fiery gaze skimmed her bare breasts. 'No wonder the Sheikh was so charmed; you virtually displayed yourself naked in that dress.'

'Please, Raul,' Penny murmured, suddenly beginning to feel frightened of him for the first time in their relationship, even as her breasts hardened under his searching gaze.

'You think I treat you like a concubine? You think I keep you as a slave? It is time you knew the difference, my sweet Penny—my sweet, innocent, flirtatious Penny,' he snarled with savage mockery. Then, bending his head, he deliberately bit down lightly on one rose-tipped breast and then the other.

Penny jerked beneath him and felt the familiar heat of instant arousal in her loins. Raul at his worst could still excite her, even as she hated herself for it. His mouth found hers and his teeth nipped at her lips until she gave him access. His tongue plunged deep into her mouth, stroking, arousing, demanding her response, and she could not deny him.

Passion ignited between them like a forest fire run wild. Raul reared back, his hand ripping her dress and panties down and off her feet, and, within seconds of discarding his trousers, he was once more over her.

His lips found hers and she was ready for him. The heat, the aroused male scent, the hard-packed muscle were her own particular aphrodisiac. She could no more resist him than stop the ocean tide. The blood pounded through her veins; she could feel the rapid pounding of his mighty heart as she pulled at his shirt, tearing off the buttons in her haste to feel his naked flesh against her breasts. Instead his mouth found her hardened peaks and suckled each in turn as one long leg parted her thighs and he slammed into her with savage ease.

It was over in a minute—a rapacious coupling that neither could resist. Raul's full weight collapsed on top of her and he buried his head on the pillow over her shoulder.

Penny, fighting for breath, was appalled at her own lack of control. But that Raul had so completely lost control that he had forgotten protection she found incredible.

'Raul,' she murmured, slipping her arm around his shoulders, her slender fingers tracing up the back of his neck and into his sweat-damp, curling hair.

He turned his head away from her; his eyes caught the flash of diamonds on the bedside table and he groaned. Moving onto his back and sweeping Penny into his arms, he said huskily, '*Dios*, I'm sorry, Penny.' His voice was deep with remorse. 'It's your birthday, and I lost it completely. Did I hurt you?'

'No. Surprised me, shocked me a little, but hurt me? Never,' Penny reassured him softly, her blue eyes gazing up into his darkly handsome face which was dazed with the aftermath of violent passion.

'I shocked myself,' Raul said with wry mockery. 'I did not believe I could feel such jealousy. Seeing that Arab kiss your hand, I suddenly wanted to hit him.'

'Hardly good business practice,' Penny teased, luxuriating in the comfort of her lover's arms and secretly delighted that Raul had been jealous. It must mean that he loved her!

'I know, and then to introduce you as my companion...I'm not surprised you were angry. I should have said partner.' And, tilting her head back, he brushed her lips with a gentle kiss.

'Partner. Yes, I like that,' she murmured, stroking her hand over his hairy chest. 'If it is true.' She glanced up through her thick lashes at his beloved face, needing all the reassurance she could get.

'Of course it is true. Now and for ever,' Raul declared throatily, his hand capturing hers on his broad chest.

Penny sighed her contentment. Raul was hers. All of him. And, glancing down at the muscular length of his magnificent body, she began to giggle.

'What's so funny?'

'Oh, Raul, the business tycoon, still wearing his jacket and shirt, admittedly torn open, then naked from the waist down except for his socks.'

Raul pulled himself up the bed and looked down. His lips twitched; he glanced at Penny and lifted a socked foot, and they both burst out laughing, the happy sound echoing in the still night air.

CHAPTER TWO

'COME on, sleepyhead; you have ten minutes to get ready.'

Penny opened her eyes and looked up at Raul standing by the side of the bed. She stretched and smiled—a slow, sensuous curve of her full lips. She lifted out a hand towards him. Then, frowning, she let it drop to the coverlet. He was already dressed in a navy silk suit...

'Not this morning, honey,' he drawled with a mocking grin, accurately reading her mind. Usually they started the day in a much more enjoyable fashion.

Penny murmured, 'Spoilsport!' and snuggled back under the cover. 'You work if you must, but I feel like another hour in bed.'

'Sorry, but there has been a change of plan.'

'What?' she asked fuzzily, reluctant to leave the warmth of the wide bed.

'Come on, Penny; move it. The honeymoon can't last for ever. You're booked on a flight back to Spain leaving in seventy minutes.'

'We're leaving?' She hauled herself up into a sitting position, her eyes flicking enquiringly to his hard face.

'Not exactly. I have to stay a few days to sort out a couple of problems with the design of the desalination plant. But you are going back to the *hacienda*; you will be safer there. I should never have brought you with me in the first place. Too many men around here would pay a fortune for a girl like you, and I cannot be around to protect you all day.'

He crossed the room and pulled back the curtains, allowing the blistering brilliance of the morning sun to illuminate the room. Penny blinked at the harsh light, and the even harsher expression on Raul's dark face.

'Really, Raul, aren't you overreacting a bit?' she responded drily. 'I can't see myself being kidnapped out of the Hyatt Regency, somehow.' And, sliding out of bed, dragging the sheet around her naked body, she crossed to where he stood lounging against the window-frame. 'And you did promise to take me to England,' she reminded him peevishly. 'I've arranged—'

'Not now, Penny; I haven't the time to argue.' He cut her off in mid-sentence. 'I don't want you here. I want you back in Spain, where Ava and Carlos can look after you.' Pushing away from the window, he swatted her bottom as he brushed past her. 'Do as you're told and hurry. You now have only eight minutes.'

The master has spoken, Penny thought angrily, but still she did as she was told. Packing took a matter of minutes, and after a lightning-fast shower she pulled on her briefs, a pair of white cotton trousers and a blue halter-top, slipped white espadrilles on her feet and she was ready. But silently simmering with resentment.

She marched into the sitting room, ready to demand an explanation. Raul knew perfectly well that she had arranged to meet her friend Amy in London at the weekend. Now he was suggesting that she stay in Spain and wait for him like a dutiful little wife. Except she wasn't his wife! And what had he said earlier? 'The honeymoon can't last for ever.'

She paused. Was that how Raul viewed the past few idyllic months that they had been together—a honeymoon for him, without the complication of having to marry the girl in the first place?

'*Dios*, Penny, are you determined to make a spectacle of yourself?' Raul's angry voice sliced the air.

'Spectacle?' She glanced up at his frowning face. What had she done wrong now?

'No bra, bare arms, bare back—is there no end to your stupidity?'

Penny looked down at her neat blue halter-top and back up at her lover's grim face. 'Apparently not,' she muttered, and she wasn't just referring to her clothes.

'No matter; you haven't time to change.' And, grabbing her arm, he bustled her out of the suite and into the waiting elevator.

'Even if I had, I wouldn't,' she snapped defiantly. 'In case you hadn't noticed, it is the middle of June, the temperature is over a hundred degrees, and it will not be much different in Andalusia. I couldn't give a fig if the women here go around covered from head to foot. I am Christian and British and will wear what I please.'

She almost added, *So there*. Much as she loved Raul, he could be the most arrogant, chauvinistic man in the world sometimes.

'Happy you got that off your chest?' Raul drawled mockingly, with a cynical, sensual glance at that particular part of her anatomy.

Penny felt the colour surge in her face but wasn't sure whether it was anger or arousal that was making her blush. 'Yes,' she snapped back, and turned her head away as he slipped one arm around her waist, his head lowering towards hers. She wasn't in the mood to kiss and make up. She was angry, confused and bitterly disappointed.

Perhaps it was just as well that they were parting for a while. The events of the last twelve hours had left an unpleasant taste in her mouth. She had glimpsed herself

through a stranger's eyes—those of an Arab prince—
and she did not like what she saw. Plus, Raul's attitude
did not help one b˙

It was as if coming to an Arab country had heightened
in him the characteristics of his Moorish forefathers. The
Moors had once dominated southern Spain for nearly
eight hundred years, and, watching Raul now, she could
quite imagine him locking her away in purdah, given
half a chance.

His home, situated west of Granada, was built in the
Moorish style—all graceful arches and elegant balconies
but with iron grilles at the windows. A central courtyard,
sheltered from the burning heat of the summer by ancient
olive and lemon trees, also effectively blocked off the
outside world.

The land had been in Raul's family for generations—
a huge estate with vast expanses of olive groves stretching
across the gently waving plains and higher up into the
hills where roamed cattle and the horses which Raul kept
as a hobby. She loved the place, but it was isolated . . .

She glanced up at him, her disturbing thoughts clearly
reflected in her blue eyes. But at that moment the elevator doors swished open and Raul straightened to his
full height, his dark face impassive as he ushered her
across the elegant foyer and out into the scorching heat
of the morning sun.

A chauffeur opened the door of a waiting limousine
and, without a word being spoken, Penny found herself
in the back seat with Raul beside her.

'I suppose I should be honoured you can actually spare
the time to take me to the airport,' Penny sniped, still
hurting at his high-handed action in shipping her back
to Spain. A long arm curved around her slender shoulder

and Raul's other hand caught her chin and turned her face towards his.

'Penny. My darling girl. Please don't be angry.' One long finger traced the outline of her mouth and a soft sigh escaped her. Why was she fighting with him? She loved him; one touch, a tender word and she ached for him.

'I'm not angry.' She smiled slightly. 'Only sad. It's just hit me that we have never spent a night apart from the day I moved in with you. I will miss you,' she confessed with blunt honesty.

Raul hugged her to him as his dark eyes caught and held hers. 'I hate for us to be apart even for one night. You must know that, honey. But I wasn't totally honest with you last night. I was furious that you met the Sheikh but it wasn't just that. The trouble at the plant was a contributing factor for my appallingly bad temper.'

'Oh, Raul, you should have confided in me. That's what partners do, you know,' she chided him gently, adding, 'I'm not dumb; you can discuss your work with me.'

'I should not have called you dumb,' he admitted, planting a brief kiss on her nose. 'Naïve, maybe, but I had no right to insult your intelligence. Only, it is hard for me, this relationship thing! I have been too many years on my own. But I will try and do better, I promise.'

His dark head bent and his mouth gently covered hers. A long, satisfying kiss followed, Raul finally ending it by easing her head back against the seat and groaning, 'I have a suspicion that kissing in public, even in a car, is against the law here.'

Penny snuggled into the curve of his broad shoulder. Once more at ease, she prompted, 'So tell me about the plant. It sometimes helps to talk out a problem with a

third party, I find.' And it might stop her thinking about
the hardness of his thigh against her own, and what she
would really like to be doing.

'Such wisdom from one so young,' he mocked, but
continued in a more serious vein. 'I was your age—
twenty-three—fresh out of university with a degree in
engineering specialising in design. I thought I would work
at a large firm in Granada and live happily at the
hacienda, helping out on the estate for the rest of my
days. Unfortunately my father died. I discovered the
ranch was mortgaged to the hilt, and that a salary,
however good, would not allow me to redeem the
mortgage in one lifetime. That is why I started my own
business—'

'I didn't realise. I simply assumed you had always been
disgustingly wealthy,' Penny interrupted teasingly.

'So did I,' he said with dry irony. 'Until I found out
different. It is only in the past ten years I have actually
been solvent. And this desalination plant in Dubai was
to be my crowning achievement.

'I designed it. It is an innovative and slightly contro-
versial design. Unfortunately one small part needs to be
rethought. I have to stay here and solve the problem,
because the rewards if I succeed are astronomical—not
solely in monetary terms but in human terms. Think of
the millions that die each year in Africa alone because
of drought, and yet in some countries the sea is there to
be used but is ignored.

'I can foresee the design being used not just in the
Middle Eastern countries but any coastal area in the
world where a shortage of water is a major problem—
including my own country.'

Penny was stunned. This was a new Raul, talking
about his life and work as he never had to her before,

and she was enormously impressed at the depth of his commitment and flattered that he had confided in her. She felt as though it marked a new phase in their relationship, increasing her belief in him and his love for her.

'So you see, Penny, much as I want to keep you with me, to be honest, I cannot afford the distraction.'

He stretched a hand across her chest to cup the underside of her breast, and she shivered in reaction, the nipple peaking blatantly beneath the soft cotton of her top. She glanced sideways at his rugged face and caught his wry smile.

'And you, *querida*, are a major distraction,' he husked throatily. 'At least if I know you are at home waiting for me I will have the incentive to work all the harder, simply to get back to you.'

It was her turn to move and press her lips to his. 'I do understand, Raul, and I will be counting the days.'

He hauled her into his arms, local laws forgotten, and kissed her thoroughly. Then he murmured against her softly parted lips, 'And I will be counting the nights. *Dios*, Penny, you must know you can ask anything of me—anything in the world—and I would move heaven and earth to get it for you.'

As an avowal of love, Penny couldn't have asked for more, and, with his words warming her heart as his kiss still lingered on her lips, fifteen minutes later she boarded the waiting aircraft. Her confidence in their love was at an all-time high... And she never imagined for a second that two weeks later the reverse would be true...

Penny slowly opened her eyes and groaned. Her sleep had been haunted by dreams; her body burning and aching with need, as she had spent a restless night in the huge four-poster bed. She glanced down at the fine cotton sheet tangled around her naked body and sighed. So this was what sexual frustration did to one, she thought grimly, and wished for the hundredth time that Raul was back.

She yawned and stretched; then, slowly untangling herself from the sheet, she swung her long legs to the floor. Raul's 'a few days' had lengthened into two weeks, and, much as she loved the *hacienda*, if she was honest with herself, after months of doing absolutely nothing she was beginning to get bored. She was slowly reaching the conclusion that she hadn't been cut out to be a lady of leisure.

A deep sigh escaped her and she sat for a moment on the side of the bed. She pushed the unruly mass of her long hair back from her face and glanced idly out of the window. Another scorching hot day, but her flesh was burning with a different heat—the heat of arousal unfulfilled.

Still, she told herself bracingly, breakfast and down to the stables for a long gallop on her own small Arab mare, Daisy—a present from Raul the first time she had stayed with him in Spain. Followed by lunch, a swim . . . Who was she trying to fool? She had done the same thing every day for weeks, and was fed up.

What would her mother have said, she mused, if she could have seen her precious daughter now, a wealthy man's mistress? Her blue eyes hazed with tears. Deep in her innermost being Penny knew the answer, and it gave her no joy. Her parents had been a wonderful loving couple; they might have tolerated her lifestyle because she was their beloved daughter, but they would never have approved in a million years.

Her thoughts went back to the past. As the much loved only child of the local doctor in a small town in West Sussex, she had had an idyllic upbringing until her father had been killed in a car crash when on a night call to an elderly patient. Even after his death she had still been relatively content; she had grown even closer to her mother and life had gone on.

It had been when she was seventeen that the final disaster had struck: her mother had been diagnosed as having cancer. A braver woman never lived, Penny thought with some pride. Her mother had insisted that Penny stay at school and take her final exams. She had been destined to follow in her father's footsteps and had been accepted for medical school.

Whether it was the worry over her mother or simply that she was not quite clever enough, she didn't know, but her exam results had not been good enough for her to take up her place. With hindsight she could see that it had been a blessing in disguise.

The local pharmacy where she had worked every Saturday since the age of fifteen had allowed her to work part-time, twenty hours a week, and she had devoted the next year to looking after her mother. Then, when the end had come and her mother died, the same firm had agreed to sponsor her through pharmaceutical college. Reluctantly she had sold the family house, bought a small apartment in London and started college.

A reminiscent smile curved her full lips. The very first day she'd met Amy, an orphan like herself, but looking for accommodation. They had shared Penny's apartment ever since. In fact Amy was still living there. Which reminded her...

She stood up and walked across to the *en suite* bathroom. She owed Amy a phone call; apart from ringing when she had first arrived back in Spain, to apologise for not keeping her appointment in London with her, she had not spoken to her friend at all.

Raul, on the other hand, had called Penny every night, but as she stepped into the shower and turned on the cold spray she seriously questioned the effect of his calls. Invariably she put the phone down in a state of sexual arousal, and she was getting heartily sick of cold showers. In fact she would have loved to know what idiot had actually decided they worked as a cure for frustration, because they did not seem to be doing her much good.

Half an hour later, after a quick cup of coffee—she could not face Ava the housekeeper's idea of a breakfast—Penny was astride Daisy, cantering along the dusty track that led to her favourite spot—a wild grove of orange and lemon trees, gnarled and old, planted decades ago by whoever had once lived in the tumbledown adobe building at the edge of the orchard. A small stream trickled by only twenty feet from the ruined home. The stream was almost dried up in the mid-summer heat, but still Penny found it soothing.

Eventually, reluctantly, she returned to the *hacienda*, groomed and fed her horse, and then made her way back to the house.

'I won't be five minutes,' she called to Ava in her rapidly improving Spanish before lightly running up the wide marble staircase. One positive thing to come out of her relationship with Raul, she thought smugly, was that, having studied Spanish as a second language at school, she had finally got a chance to use it, and had discovered that she had a remarkable aptitude for the melodious tongue.

Nipping into the shower, she had a quick wash, then dried herself and dressed equally quickly in a pair of brief white cotton shorts and a plain white shirt, which she didn't bother fastening, simply tying the ends together under her breasts before slipping on a pair of soft leather mules and leaving the bedroom.

The sound of the doorbell ringing made her hesitate for a second on the top step of the wide staircase. In the many times she had stayed here, there had been few visitors. The ones that did call when Raul was around Penny rarely met. The thought made her pause, and she frowned, wondering who it could be.

Penny heard the voice before she saw the unexpected guest. And she knew enough Spanish to stiffen in outrage.

'My God, I thought Raul would have got rid of you and that useless husband of yours by now, Ava. Tell your master I'm here and fetch me a drink. I'll be in the salon.'

Penny ran down the stairs, taking in the scene before her at a glance. Ava was standing by the open front door, her face a picture of hurt surprise and disgust, her kindly old eyes fixed in horror on the girl marching past her.

The young woman was small, dark and looked as though she had just stepped out of *Vogue*. From her perfectly coiffured black hair piled on top of her head to the elegant high-heeled shoes that tapped out a staccato tune across the mosaic floor she looked like a woman who owned all she surveyed.

'Excuse me; can I help you?' Penny said frostily, stepping in front of the stranger. Close up, it was obvious that the woman was older than Penny had first thought—mid-thirties, maybe.

'I very much doubt it. It is Raul I have come to visit. Now get out of my way and tell that stupid old woman to fetch me a white wine.'

Anger turned Penny's cool face to bright scarlet in seconds. She had never in her life met such an ill-mannered, arrogant woman and she acted without thought of the consequences.

'Raul is not here, nor is he likely to be for some time. In his absence I am in charge and I suggest you leave immediately. Ava is the housekeeper here and she is not employed to put up with insults from uninvited guests.'

'How dare you talk to me like that? I am Dulciana Maria Costas; my father is a government minister.'

'Well, he should have taught you some manners. Now, if you don't mind, Ava will show you out.'

The perfectly made-up face twisted with rage. 'Raul will hear of this, you little English whore. I have heard all about you—Raul's latest bed-mate. If you have any sense you will pack up and leave now. Once Raul knows I am back he will have no further use for you. That I can promise.'

Penny went from red to white to red again, with a mixture of fury and not a little embarrassment. 'Get out,' she spluttered.

'I will leave—but I will be back. And if you have any sense you will take my advice. Do yourself a favour and save yourself total humiliation.' And, spinning on her heel, the arrogant Dulciana Maria Costas marched back out of the front door.

Penny sat down on the bottom step of the stairs, her trembling legs refusing to support her. 'Who on earth was that witch of woman, Ava?' she asked, glancing across at the older lady.

'Dulciana Costas; her father is in the government, but he also happens to own the adjoining ranch.'

Penny got to her feet. 'So I have just insulted our nearest neighbour.' She grimaced and caught an unexpected flash of sympathy in Ava's dark eyes.

'I am honoured you came to my defence, Penny, but I wish you hadn't for your sake. Dulcie Costas is a bad lady to cross.'

'She can't harm me.' Penny shrugged with more nonchalance than she actually felt.

'I'm not so sure,' Ava responded, with a worried shake of her grey head. 'Come.' Gesturing with one hand for Penny to follow her, she walked through an open door at one side of the hall, through the splendid dining room and out into the central courtyard.

'I have set lunch in the courtyard, and while you eat I will explain.'

'Explain what?' Penny asked, sinking down on the wrought-iron chair at the beautifully set small table. The selection of attractively displayed cold meats and salads suddenly made her realise how hungry she was. She loaded her plate with chicken, ham and a lot of crisp green salad. 'Do sit down, Ava, instead of hovering; I've told you before I don't need you to wait on me.'

Ava sighed and murmured, 'Perhaps this once.' And, pulling out the opposite chair, she sat down primly on the edge.

'So who is this Dulcie? Why all the mystery and heavy sighs?' Penny demanded, swallowing a mouthful of chicken.

'First, I wish to apologise that when you first arrived with Master Raul I was disapproving. Never had Raul brought a lady to this house to sleep in his bed. I am old; the modern times have passed me by. But very soon I realised he is in love with you, and you with him. I think you will marry and the *hacienda* will once again echo to the sound of laughter and children's voices.'

'I sincerely hope so,' Penny said, blushing scarlet but delighted that Ava was confirming her own heartfelt belief.

'I have never seen Raul so happy. I have known him all his life—as a baby, a young boy and as a man. I know him better than he knows himself. If he has one fault it is that he is fearful of committing himself to a woman. I do not usually gossip but I think you are entitled to know what makes him the way he is.'

Penny stopped eating and, picking up the carafe of white wine from the centre of the table, filled her glass, and, lifting it to her mouth, took a sip, her eyes fixed in fascination on Ava.

'Go on,' she prompted eagerly.

'Raul was eight years old when his mother ran off with an American serviceman stationed in Spain. His father was devastated—never really recovered. Poor Raul did not understand what had happened or why his mother never came to see him again. I tried my best to take his mother's place, but by the time he was a teenager he was very bitter. His father didn't help by repeatedly cursing young women, and his mother in particular.'

'How awful.' Penny sighed, her tender heart full of sympathy for Raul as a lonely young boy.

'True, but worse was to follow. You have met Dulcie; you have seen what she is like. Well, with the families being neighbours it was inevitable that Dulcie became Raul's "friend", for want of a better word. Raul went off to university in America, but they corresponded and eventually became betrothed.

'It suited both parents, and Raul was used to looking after the girl. But I had my doubts. Dulcie was totally spoilt by an over-indulgent father, and when Raul was studying Dulcie was off to Paris, Rome—anywhere there were men and money. The rumours were rife and *true*, but Raul never suspected.'

Penny's mind reeled. Raul had been engaged to the woman she had thrown out of his home. She couldn't believe it. He had once loved that witch of a woman and yet had never mentioned it to her. Did she know him at all? She listened with mounting disquiet as Ava went on.

'The wedding date had already been fixed when Raul's father died and everything changed. Dulcie discovered that Raul's father had died in debt and that there was no money to support her extravagant lifestyle, and a month before the wedding she took off with a Colombian cattle baron—though some said his business was more chemical than cattle...

'Apparently the Colombian traded her in for a younger, more fertile model, and she returned to Spain two days ago. I am telling you all this, Penny, so you are warned. The master loves you and, given time, he will marry you—of this I am sure. But beware of Dulcie; she is an evil but clever woman. Around the master she was always sweet and innocent, but you have seen how she treats people when he is not around.'

For some reason all Penny could think of was Raul and that horrid woman together. She was eaten alive with jealousy at the thought of Raul making love to Dulcie, touching the other woman as he now touched her. It was ridiculous; it had all been over years ago but she could not help feeling a certain dread. She tried a smile.

'Don't worry, Ava. Raul is much older and wiser; he would never allow himself to be fooled twice, and—'

'So this is how my two favourite women spend their time when I am not around.' A deep laughing voice cut across Penny's. 'Drinking wine and gossiping.'

Penny spun around in her chair. It was Raul… He was leaning carelessly against the wood frame of the dining-room door, his jacket casually hooked on a long finger and draped over one broad shoulder. A snowy white shirt open at the neck revealed the strong column of his tanned throat, and his eyes glinted with humour and something more. He looked all male and incredibly sexy. Penny jumped to her feet and in seconds had thrown herself at him.

His arms opened to enfold her. 'You never said last night.' She reached up and raked her fingers through his dark hair, cradling his head with her small hands. Her head tilted back to gaze up into his handsome face.

'I decided to surprise you, *querida*,' he murmured as his mouth fastened on hers.

CHAPTER THREE

RAUL'S kiss was so overpowering that Penny was lost in it in seconds; she forgot where they were and that they had an audience; she hungered for him with a desperation she had not thought possible. Once more in his arms, her tongue twining with his, she clawed unconsciously at the fine silk of his shirt, popping his buttons in her haste to feel the satin skin beneath, while Raul's hands roamed freely down her back, cupping her buttocks, hauling her into the hard cradle of his hips, making her intimately aware of his aroused state.

'*Dios*,' he groaned against her mouth, and when he lifted his head, his dark gaze burned down into the blue depths of her passion-glazed eyes. 'That was some welcome, Penny. Can I take it you missed me, hmm?'

'Yes, every minute,' she agreed, an ecstatic smile lighting her lovely face.

'Did you miss anything else?' he demanded hardly, straightening to his full height and stepping back.

'Only you.' She moved and, standing on tiptoe, nipped at his square jaw. It was as high as she could reach. His strong hands curved around her shoulders, holding her firmly away from him, and through the euphoric haze at seeing him again it slowly dawned on Penny that he was deliberately keeping her at a distance.

'Raul?' she husked tentatively as his dark eyes slid down the length of her body with a possessive arrogance, then back to her flushed face, a silent demand in their black depths. Wide, puzzled blue eyes met his nar-

39

rowed, predatory gaze and a tremor of something very like fear slithered down her spine. Raul exuded a raw, animal magnetism, an aura of power and vitality that suddenly seemed oddly threatening. And what on earth did he mean? Who else could she have missed? It didn't make sense.

'You're sure about that?' he queried, the corner of his mouth twisting in a cynical smile.

'Of course,' she said emphatically. Surely he knew how much she'd missed him, loved him…? 'What is it, Raul? What's wrong?' She twisted her hand in his shirt in agitation and another button popped.

'Nothing—nothing at all. But unless you want to shock poor Ava completely—' his hands dropped to catch hers at his chest, and, entwining their fingers, he lowered her hands to her sides '—I think you'd better stop trying to rip my shirt off.' His dark head bent, and, his voice lowering to a husky drawl, he added, 'Not that I mind. I seem to remember denying you a siesta in Dubai; now seems a good time to correct the omission.'

She had forgotten all about the older woman. Penny glanced over her shoulder to see Ava standing by the table, her brown eyes wide and round and ever so slightly shocked. 'I think you're right.' She turned back to Raul, her lips twitching. 'We don't want to offend her sensibilities, and suddenly I feel incredibly tired.' She chuckled, inwardly relieved that it was only Ava's presence inhibiting Raul, and nothing more sinister.

Penny opened her eyes and yawned widely. The sun was setting, the last rays streaking the room with a warm rosy light. She turned on her side and smiled, a languorous sexy curl to her mouth as her gaze feasted on Raul lying flat on his back beside her. His chest rose and fell slowly in the steady rhythm of sleep.

With his eyes closed he looked younger and somehow vulnerable. The ridiculously long sweep of his dark lashes curved on his high cheekbones, almost feminine in their thick lusciousness. But it was certainly the only slightly feminine thing about him, Penny thought dreamily, and, raising up on one elbow, she studied his sprawling, nude body.

They had spent all afternoon in bed and had finally fallen into an exhausted sleep. Now just looking at Raul made her shiver with the rekindling of passion. She reached out a small hand and ran it lightly over his broad shoulder and across his massive chest, her fingers entwining in the surprisingly soft chest hair. She grazed a small male nipple and still her hand moved down.

It was incredibly sweet to have him at her mercy, to let her hand roam lower over the taut, flat stomach, to feel his hard, warm body, to linger over the muscles of his thighs. She lowered her head and kissed him softly, not wanting to wake him, simply to love him freely with her hands and mouth.

'Woman, behave.' Raul's hand grasped her wrist like a manacle and in seconds their positions were reversed. Penny was flat on her back and Raul was looking down into her startled eyes. 'You're insatiable,' he chuckled. 'I never imagined when I first took you to bed what a sleeping tiger I was arousing.'

'Tigress, surely?' she husked, shivering in delight as his glittering dark eyes swept her naked body with a sensuous, knowing triumph. 'You're the only tiger around here, with your gold-flecked eyes,' she corrected him throatily.

'Grr...' Raul teased, and, bending, rubbed his un-shaven jaw against her soft cheek. 'Only around you, Penny.' He lifted his head. 'You must know I adore you.'

She sighed as his hand trailed across her body to cup one full, round breast. 'And I you; all you have to do is touch me and you can have m-e-e-e.' She ended on a moan as he rolled one taut nipple between his thumb and finger, sending arrows of sensation through her ultra-sensitive flesh.

'Much as I would like to take up your offer, I can't.' He brushed his mouth briefly over hers. 'I have work to do if I am to take you to London at the weekend.'

Penny beamed up at him. 'You mean that?'

'Yes. I promised and I am a man of my word.' He rolled over and got to his feet, and she stared at him, her breath catching in her throat.

At that moment she loved him more than life. Raul, her lover, was back. How could she have imagined for a second that she was bored? She would spend her life waiting for Raul if she had to, but she didn't need to. He was here and he was keeping his promise to take her to London. He did love her. Ava was right; it was only a matter of time before they married.

Her loving gaze roamed over him and a surprised gasp escaped her as he turned and smiled down at her, mag-nificent in his nudity. Contrary to what he had said, he could not hide his body's readiness to take up her offer.

'It isn't so shocking,' he said, his voice deep and tinged with laughter as he caught her wayward gaze. 'My body might be weak but my mind is strong, and I do have some calls to make.'

She lifted her eyes to his. 'I think you might have got that quote the wrong way around.' She let her glance slide back down the long, hard length of him. 'Weak is hardly an accurate description from where I am,' she joked.

'Tigress.' And lips twitching, Raul bent down and brushed a cheeky kiss across the twin peaks of her full breasts. 'Get up, get a shower and put something pretty on this sexy body that won't distract me. Then come downstairs, and after we have eaten we'll talk.' Swinging on his heel, he walked off.

Penny sighed happily and, turning on her stomach, savoured the lingering scent of Raul and love on the crumpled sheets. She heard him moving around, dressing, but was too sated and lazy to move.

For the next few days Penny thought that life was perfect... They shared breakfast in the secluded courtyard and then Raul locked himself in the study for the morning, but after lunch he was all hers.

They spent an afternoon in the marvellous old city of Granada in the foothills of the Sierra Nevada. They strolled hand in hand around the Alhambra palace, built for the Moorish rulers hundreds of years earlier.

Penny gazed in awestruck wonder at the ostentatious luxury. The walls carved with swirls of ornate stucco, the tons of white marble and coloured glass, and the ceilings, hand-carved from cedarwood, designed to represent heaven, almost convinced her that she was already there!

Later, sharing a picnic, which had been lovingly supplied by Ava, in the gardens where the constant splash of running water and dripping fountains lent a pleasant coolness to the air, Penny smiled at Raul's reclining figure and was convinced. Heaven could not possibly be better...

*   *   *

Singing happily to herself, Penny descended the grand staircase. She had finished the packing, and at nine o'clock the next morning they would be on a flight out of Alicante, arriving in London Friday lunchtime. She had called Amy and arranged to call at the apartment on Sunday, to catch up on the news.

She was dressed in a simple green silk slip of a gown, tiny straps supporting the soft fabric that clung loosely to her lithe body, the hemline ending just above her knees to reveal her long, shapely legs. On her feet delicate wedge-heeled gold and green sandals glittered as she skipped lightly down the stairs.

She had left her blonde hair loose to curl enticingly over her shoulders and down her back because she knew that Raul preferred it that way. She was totally unaware of how stunning she looked. The glow of love had given her fine features an incandescent beauty, her softly swollen lips needed no lipstick, and her blue eyes sparkled with the inner radiance of a woman who knew she was loved.

'Penelope.' The voice was harsh.

Penny's foot hesitated on the bottom step of the stairs; her heart thumped in her breast. Raul was standing in the entrance, elegantly dressed in a dark business suit, the sun behind him outlining his huge frame in a halo of fire. For a second he looked like the devil incarnate. His business meeting must have finished early, she thought inconsequentially.

'Raul, you're back.' She moved towards him, a tentative smile pulling at her wide mouth.

'Too late, it would seem, to stop your idiocy,' he drawled scathingly.

'My idiocy?' She shook her head, her fair hair floating around her naked shoulders. What on earth was he talking about? Her eyes searched his rugged face and she shivered inside.

'Don't play the blue-eyed innocent with me, Penny. I'm too old to be fooled.' And the contempt in his voice flicked her like a whiplash.

'Please, Raul.' She lifted her hand to his chest but he swept her aside.

'In my study... *now.*'

She followed him. Noting the tension in his broad back, she chewed nervously at her bottom lip. Something had upset him, but what?

She had barely put a foot in the oak-panelled study before he turned on her, and, slamming the door behind her, he rested one hand on the hard wood and stared down into her confused face. But this was not the man who had left her a handful of hours earlier. His dark eyes were as hard as jet, and as unyielding.

'What the hell have you been doing, woman?' he demanded icily.

'P-p-packing,' she stammered, totally intimidated by the cold rage in his dark eyes.

'Don't be facetious; it does not suit you.'

'I...' Trapped against the door, with his huge body towering over her, Penny touched the tip of her tongue to her dry lips. 'I wasn't—'

'Who on earth gave you the right to insult my neighbours, to order a friend from my house in my absence?'

She felt the colour drain from her face. She stared at him helplessly. The shock of being confronted in such a way by the man she loved was totally numbing.

'How dared you do such a thing?' A cruel smile twisted across his face. 'On what authority?'

'On what authority'. The words echoed in her brain. They were lovers, partners—or so she had thought. Ob-

viously Raul's idea of a partnership was not the same
as hers.

Angry colour flooded Penny's cheeks. The nerve of
the man, yelling at her as if she were no more than a
servant in his home. Not even that—he was unfailingly
polite to Ava and Carlos. What was the matter with her?
She was letting Raul intimidate her yet again, as he had
in the beginning when she had mentioned marriage, and
again in Dubai, when he had packed her off to Spain.
Was she a woman or a doormat? she asked herself.

Her spine stiffening, she looked straight into his dark,
furious eyes. 'I was under the impression that we were
partners, and in your absence I was to treat your house
as my own,' she said, her voice coolly measured in sharp
contrast to her rapidly beating heart. 'If I misunderstood you, I'm sorry.'

A dark flush covered his hard face and he had the
grace to look ashamed at his outburst, but not for long...
'Yes, yes, but not to the extent of insulting my neighbours.' He stormed across the room and then swung back
to face her, running his large hand through his dark hair
in angry frustration. 'You will have to apologise to
Dulcie, not me.'

'I presume you are referring to that hateful woman,
Dulciana Maria Costas. She marched into the house and
was unspeakably rude to poor Ava. I told her to leave,
as any other right-minded person would have done, and
if you think for a second I will apologise to the woman
forget it.' Penny glared at him and folded her arms across
her chest.

His mouth thinned to a hard line. 'Dulcie does not
speak English. How do you know what was said?' he
sneeringly demanded.

'Because my Spanish is good; I understood perfectly and acted accordingly.'

'Nonsense, Penny, you must have misunderstood. I have known Dulcie all my life. Unlike you, she would not deliberately insult anyone,' he said with cutting sarcasm.

'Obviously you have no such qualms,' she shot back, but his words bruised her heart. Nonsensical was she? Along with 'dumb' and 'idiocy' it all added up to a man who had no respect for her as a person. Suddenly with blinding clarity she recognised what she had become. From an intelligent, ambitious woman she had turned into a fool for love. She blinked rapidly to hold back the tears, not sure if they were tears of sorrow or pure rage.

She shook her head in disbelief, and stared at Raul as though she had never seen him before. 'How could you take the word of an old fiancée you have not seen for years against mine?'

'I see Ava has been gossiping.' One dark brow arched sardonically. 'I might have guessed. You saw Dulcie as a rival and were smitten by the green-eyed god. Really, Penny, how childish.'

He could not have said anything more likely to enrage her. Childish was she? And jealous, to boot! She had not known who the damn woman was in the first place.

'Rubbish! I didn't even know the woman was your ex-fiancée until later. You certainly never mentioned her,' she spat back, her body tense with outrage and a deepening hurt that she did her best to disguise.

'My past relationships are none of your business,' Raul informed her with icy precision. 'It is the present that concerns you, and in half an hour Señor Costas and his daughter will be arriving for dinner.'

Penny's mouth fell open in surprise and she spluttered, 'You invited...?' She could not go on, she was so furious, her body rigid with the effort to control her rage.

'Yes. And I expect you to apologise for your behaviour the other day, and, hopefully, we can enjoy a civilised meal.' She caught the implacable expression in his eyes, and her breath stopped in her throat as she realised what he had said.

Slowly she moved towards him, her cheeks scarlet, her anger so livid that she was shaking with it. She registered the arrogant stance of his tall body, the hands tucked easily into the pockets of his trousers.

Every inch the Spanish grandee, master in his own home, he exuded an aura of power and raw masculine sex appeal that could not be ignored. It was inherent in his every move and gesture. But for once Penny refused to succumb to his lethal appeal; instead she stopped a few inches in front of him and deliberately raised her gaze to his hard face, her blue eyes flashing with fury.

'Over—my—dead—body.' She dropped each word slowly into the tense silence. 'I would not apologise to that woman to save my life,' she added for good measure.

Raul shrugged. 'We will see about that.' And he smiled condescendingly. 'You're overwrought at the moment.' Taking his hand from his pocket, he casually ran one long finger down her burning cheek. 'I need to get changed. We will continue this discussion later.'

He tilted her chin up to study her flushed and furious face. 'And you'd better change into something more appropriate.' His narrowed gaze slid from her face to where the gentle curve of her full breasts was displayed by the scoop neck of her dress. 'Something that covers you slightly more than this.' His hand fell from her chin to the neckline of her dress.

'I will not do it,' she said tightly. 'I won't.' Her skin was on fire where he touched it, her heart racing with a mixture of anger and arousal.

'So the young tigress has decided to show her claws,' he drawled silkily, his finger dipping below the soft fabric to graze the dark rose areola of her breast. She shivered and Raul laughed, knowing just how he affected her.

'Don't even think about defying me, Penny; you can't win.' Pushing his hand back in his trouser pocket, he added, 'I refuse to argue with you; we are simply wasting time.' Her refusal dismissed as lightly as he would swat a fly, he continued, 'Tell Ava there will be four for dinner.' And, brushing past her, he strode confidently out of the room.

She was left trembling and weak, watching his departing back. He thought that he had won, one touch and she melted. But not this time, Penny silently vowed. She had willingly compromised her own moral values to be with Raul, but she refused to swallow her pride and self-respect and apologise when she did not believe that she was in the wrong.

Penny stared at her reflection in the dressing-table mirror. Not bad, she told herself firmly. The redness around her eyes, from the tears she had shed in the shower, was virtually unnoticeable.

Thank God she still kept her clothes in the guest bedroom. The first night she had arrived in Spain, in the interests of propriety, Raul had shown her to this room. Not that she had ever slept in it, and Ava had soon been in no doubt of their relationship because there were too many mornings when, on serving coffee to the master, she had found them together.

Tonight Penny was grateful for the privacy. She heard the doorbell ring and slowly stood up. She smoothed the soft blue jersey silk down over her slender hips and smiled at her reflection. The dress was demure, a simple swath of fabric cut straight across her shoulders, with long, narrow sleeves to her wrists, the straight skirt falling to her feet with a small fan-pleat in the back to allow the wearer to walk easily.

She turned her back and looked over her shoulder and deliberately winked at herself. The back of the gown was virtually non-existent, swooping down in a soft curve to her bottom. She lifted a small hand to her head and curled a single tendril of blonde hair around her finger. She had piled her hair up in a soft chignon and allowed a few wispy curls to tease her neck and the side of her cheeks.

On three-inch-heeled black strappy shoes she walked regally out of the room. Penny was heartily sick of being told what to do. No mini-skirts. Cover herself. Apologise. She would show Raul, she thought determinedly. She was not about to be intimidated by him or anyone else any more...

Dinner was a disaster!

Señor Costas was a small, dark, overweight lecher, Penny decided within minutes of meeting him.

Raul introduced them with, 'Dulcie you know, I believe, Penny, and this is her father, the Minister for the Environment, Señor Costas.' Urging Penny forward, he placed his hand on her back.

She held out her hand and the old man immediately lifted it to his mouth and plonked a wet kiss on it. His tongue touching her skin made her cringe. She tried to withdraw her hand but he held onto it far too long. She shot a sideways glance at Raul and then wished she hadn't; the fury in his narrowed eyes was directed all at her. He had noticed the plunging back of her dress and was not amused.

'You are a lucky man, Raul, to have such a beautiful young companion.' Señor Costas leered, and Penny felt the swift colour rise in her face. She turned to Raul, her blue eyes unconsciously pleading. He caught her glance and stroked his hand up her back in a consoling gesture, but his dark eyes remained coldly remote.

'I know, Miguel. Penny is—' But before he could finish Dulcie cut in.

'Really, Papa, it is bad manners to comment,' she simpered coyly, and, grabbing Raul's arm, urged him towards the dining room. 'Raul, darling, I'm starving, and I can't wait to taste dear Ava's food again.'

Penny had to stifle a gasp of outrage at the other woman's hypocrisy. Silently fuming at the way Dulcie was clinging to Raul, Penny reluctantly took Costas's offered arm and followed the other two.

Her blue eyes flashed with impotent fury as Raul walked to the head of the rectangular table, his dark head bent attentively to the other woman. And then he straightened up and laughed out loud. His dark eyes connected with Penny's for a second, a subtle warning in their depths, and she felt like hitting him.

But worse was to follow. Dulcie sat on Raul's right, Penny on his left, but unfortunately with Señor Costas beside her. The ensuing two hours were agony for Penny. The old man flirted shamelessly with her, along with asking a million questions about her family and future which she found almost impossible to answer. To make matters worse, all the time Dulcie monopolised Raul completely.

Finally, as Ava cleared away the main course and Costas tried to put his hand on Penny's thigh for the third time, she lost her cool and kicked the old goat firmly on the shin under the table. He yelped, and Penny hid her grin with a hand to her mouth and a contrived cough. The dirty old man had only got what he deserved.

Raul turned at the noise, his dark eyes flashing suspiciously to Penny then to Señor Costas. 'Everything all right, Miguel?' he asked solicitously.

'Yes, yes, of course, dear boy. Ava has excelled herself; the meal was excellent.'

'Good. I'm glad you're enjoying it.' Raul's narrowed eyes settled on Penny's flushed face.

'And you, Penny—I trust you are not feeling insulted by our speaking solely in Spanish.'

It was a bit late to ask now, she thought angrily, after ignoring her for almost the whole of the meal. 'Not at all.' She met his hard eyes, her own flashing fire. 'I have a good knowledge of your tongue.' She drawled the last word sensually, leaving no doubt about the *double entendre*.

'It is so nice you can speak a little Spanish,' Dulcie inserted, and, glancing coyly up at Raul, added, 'But, Raul, you should have told the poor girl that she speaks with a peasant's accent—probably with gossiping so much to Ava.'

'I rather like Penny's accent,' Raul said shortly.

Penny shouted, Hurrah, under her breath; at least he had deigned to support her in something...

'But you are so easygoing, Raul; that is what I have always loved about you,' Dulcie said softly. 'I only wish my ex-husband had had half of your sensitivity, and then maybe I would not have felt compelled to walk out on him. He was a brute,' she murmured, lifting a crystal glass of red wine and taking a small sip. Then, fixing Penny with her spiteful eyes, she added, 'You're lucky to have Raul as your...' she deliberately hesitated '...friend, Penny. I had no one. I had to make my escape from my husband all on my own.'

Penny was livid; she had sat and listened to insult upon insult and she was not about to take any more. 'Oh? As I understood it, I thought he left you for a younger woman.'

'Penelope,' Raul said harshly, 'I don't think Dulcie's marriage is a suitable subject for discussion around the dinner table.'

'I didn't bring it up. She did,' Penny shot back.

'No, really, Raul, I don't mind,' a simpering Dulcie whispered. 'It is hard to admit one has made a mistake. But when one does—' the small dark head lifted and her narrowed gaze, flashing hatred, settled on Penny '—one should leave immediately, I think.' And with a complete change of expression, her black eyes wide and dewy, she glanced up at Raul. 'Don't you agree, Raul?'

'Yes, of course.' He cast Penny a furious warning look and then smiled down at Dulcie, patting her hand comfortingly.

Penny saw red. She wasn't bitchy by nature but this woman really rubbed her up the wrong way. So, plastering a false smile on her face, she looked straight at Dulcie. 'But wasn't it hard leaving your children behind? I mean, you were married for fourteen years, I believe; they can't be very old.'

She knew damn well that the woman had no family, but she was pig-sick of sitting taking all the flak from Raul, the devious Dulcie and the lecherous old man beside her. If this was an example of Raul's friends she was glad that he hadn't introduced her to any of them before.

Raul's hand stretched out to curl around Penny's wrist, supposedly in a tender gesture, but she could feel the fingers digging into her flesh, and she knew that he was absolutely furious, but she did not care. She deliberately ignored him. Instead she took a long swig of red wine from her glass and concentrated her pseudo-sympathetic gaze upon Dulcie.

'Thank God I decided to wait before having children,' Dulcie sighed dramatically. 'As it turned out, it was a very wise decision.' She turned enormous dark eyes back up to Raul. 'I know you agree, Raul.'

Penny would have liked to hear Raul's reply, but at that moment Ava entered with a magnificent sweet on a silver serving dish—a perfect pyramid of profiteroles covered with black chocolate and decorated with luscious strawberries.

Señor Costas clapped his hands together in delight, obviously deciding to play the diplomat, so the rest of them followed suit, which meant that Penny got her wrist back from Raul's tenacious grasp. Then Señor Costas took over the conversation with a question to Raul about Dubai, and while all four ate their dessert the talk was all business.

Penny was just beginning to think that she might get through the meal with no further trouble when, with the sweet dishes cleared, Dulcie put her oar in again.

'That was a superb meal, Raul; I can't tell you how pleased I am we are all friends again—especially after that little misunderstanding the other day.' Once more the witch fixed her beady eyes on Penny.

Raul glanced at Penny, an explicit command in his dark eyes. She stared back at him in mute defiance. There was no way she was going to comment on Dulcie's statement.

Raul's lips thinned and, turning to Dulcie, he said, 'Yes, well, Penny had no idea who you were and she was really sorry about that later.' And, slowly turning his black head, he stared at Penny's red face. 'Weren't you, dear?' he prompted smoothly.

For a long, tense moment silence reigned; Penny glanced around the three people all watching her with varying degrees of anticipation. Slowly she rose to her feet, pushing back her chair.

'Please excuse me...' She saw the flash of triumph in Raul and Dulcie's eyes; they actually imagined that she was about to apologise. Well, they were in for a hell of a shock, she thought mutinously, and, forcing a broad smile to her stiff lips, added, 'I'm rather tired. But don't let me spoil your evening; I'm sure you three have plenty to catch up on.' It was a deliberate snub, but she didn't give a damn!

She saw in her peripheral vision Raul beginning to get to his feet, rigid with anger, but she forestalled whatever comment he intended making with, 'No, Raul, don't get up for me. I'll go and tell Ava to serve the coffee.' Shoving the chair back under the table, she added, 'Goodnight, Señor Costas, Dulcie.' And, turning her back on them, she walked out.

Ava turned from the stove as Penny entered the kitchen. 'I didn't hear the bell,' she said with a worried frown.

'Relax, Ava; no one rang it. But you can serve the coffee and cognac now. Only three.' It took every ounce of will power she possessed to speak normally in Spanish

to Ava when what she really wanted to do was scream
and bawl her fury and frustration at the injustice of it
all. 'I'm going to have a cup here, and if any one asks
I've gone to bed.'

'But *señorita*, you can't—'

'But I have, Ava. Please, no questions, not now.' And,
slumping down on a plain pine ladder-backed chair, she
rested her elbows on the scrubbed pine table and put her
head in her hands.

She knew that she had been incredibly rude, but then
she had been forced to share a table with two dinner
guests from hell... And what of Raul? He had been no
support. Instead he had attempted to manipulate her into
an apology that he knew perfectly well she had no intention of making.

The door opened and she lifted her head. It was Ava.
'Everything all right?' Penny asked quietly.

'They are drinking the coffee, but as for the rest... I
have never seen the master look so angry. What on earth
happened?'

Penny got to her feet and crossed to the worktop,
where a multitude of dirty dishes were scattered. 'I'll
give you a hand with clearing up, Ava.'

'But what did you do?'

'It was what I would not do that caused the problem,'
Penny said drily, and as they worked side by side, loading
the dishwasher and scrubbing the pans, Penny told Ava
the whole story.

'You should not have argued with the master because
of me,' Ava said when Penny had finished. 'And I did
warn you about Dulcie.'

'You are not paid to gossip about my life.' Raul's
furious comment cut through the air over the rattling
of dishes.

Both women turned in unison, flushed and looked decidedly guilty.

'Go to bed, Ava,' Raul ordered, his dark eyes flashing fire, and, striding towards Penny, he added, 'I want to talk to Penelope.'

Ava, with one fearful glance at Raul and a pitying one at Penny, scurried out of the room, leaving Penny with her back to the bench-top and nowhere to go as Raul clamped his hands on her shoulders and dragged her towards him.

Changing to English he bit out, 'No one, but no one makes me look a fool in my own home.' His hard mouth narrowed to a grim line as he battled to contain his rage.

'You made a fool of yourself.' She tried to defy him, and lifted her hands to push him away, to put some space between them. But he crushed her to him, his head swooping down, his mouth covering hers in a brutal, savaging kiss—a parody of what a kiss should be.

She felt as if she was drowning; she could not breathe. Her lips were pushed back against her teeth and his hands were digging into her flesh. She beat his chest with her fists and kicked out with one foot, catching him a hefty blow on the shin, which finally brought him to his senses.

He lifted his head, his glittering eyes narrowed on her bruised mouth. 'It was either kiss you or kill you. Why, Penny? Why? What satisfaction does it give you to defy me?'

His hands squeezed her shoulders; her head fell back and she stared up at his harsh face. She saw the barely restrained anger and the enquiry in his expression. In that moment she recognised that Raul honestly did not understand her at all. She took a deep, calming breath. She hated to argue with him; perhaps if she tried to explain, coolly, calmly...

'Raul, it was never my intention to make you look foolish; you did that yourself. I told you over and over again that I would not apologise to that woman.' She could not say the name. 'I know you don't believe me, but I swear she was absolutely horrible to Ava. Ask Ava if you don't believe me.'

'Ava's hearing is not that good. I suppose it never occurred to you that you might be wrong, you might be mistaken. Oh, no! You have to behave like the spoilt child you are,' he derided harshly.

'So my Spanish is no good and poor Ava is deaf.' All thoughts of staying cool deserted her; bitter bile rose in her throat and she had to swallow hard before she could continue. 'Well, at least I know where I stand.'

She was nothing to Raul—never had been. Now she knew why he had never introduced her to any of his friends; he thought of her as a spoilt child, an immature young woman good enough to go to bed with but nothing more. When it came to the crunch, and she needed his trust and support, his first allegiance was not to her.

'Yes. As an honoured guest in my house. And, as such, I expect you to behave with a modicum of good manners. Surely that is not too much to ask?' Raul said silkily, his voice hardening as he went on. 'I give you everything you want and I demand some loyalty in return. Instead of which you insult my oldest friends.'

Penny shook with temper and the fury of humiliation. 'You demand loyalty!' she shot back, and, further incensed at his arrogance, nothing could stop her from telling him a few home truths. 'It is OK for your ex-fiancée to walk all over Ava and insult me. ''English whore'' was the phrase your lady-friend used.' She laughed harshly, without humour. 'Her old goat of a father can spend all evening trying to squeeze my thigh and I am supposed to apologise to that lot simply to humour you.'

She didn't see the shocked horror in his eyes because before he could take another swipe at her crumbling self-esteem she shoved blindly past him and walked straight to the door. She paused at the entrance and looked back to where Raul was standing, a wealth of emotions flitting across his rugged features. 'Sorry. I am not into self-debasement—not even for you, Raul. Goodnight.'

CHAPTER FOUR

'FOR heaven's sake, Penny! Will you stop pacing the floor and chewing your fingernails and sit down?' Amy said, exasperation lacing her friendly voice. 'I have told you all my news, but Tanya will be back in an hour and you have still not even begun to tell me what is wrong.'

Penny sighed and collapsed onto the battered sofa next to her friend. Tanya had been sharing the apartment with Amy in Penny's absence. Apparently she was a final-year student and had met and fallen madly in love with Mike, who owned the apartment above. The happy couple were getting married in ten days' time.

'Getting married' were emotive words for Penny in her fragile state... She looked at Amy—small and slight, with a mass of wild ginger hair, her hazel eyes soft with concern—and tried to smile confidently. Amy had always been the sensitive one and Penny the practical one. How had it all changed?

'There's nothing much to tell, Amy. Raul was supposed to travel with me on Friday, but something came up at the last minute and he couldn't. He called me last night; maybe in a day or two...' Her voice trailed off.

If only it were that simple... After walking out of the kitchen on Thursday night she had gone to the guest room and undressed. Maybe she had hoped that Raul would follow her and everything would be back to normal, but he hadn't.

Instead the next morning he had coldly told her that he had to stay on in Spain a little longer. He was keen to win a government contract to build a desalination plant in southern Spain and needed to discuss the project with Costas; it was the old man's department handling the tenders. The unspoken implication had been that Penny's attitude to Costas and his daughter had not helped.

She had felt guilty and tried to apologise. Raul had dismissed her apology with a curt, 'Not important.' But when he'd added that Mrs Grimble, the caretaker of his London apartment, was expecting her, and that she was to wait there until he arrived, she was somewhat reassured. Until they reached the airport... However hard she tried she could not fool herself into believing that his goodbye kiss had been anything more than duty, not desire.

'This is Amy you're talking to, remember? You can't fool me; you're as thin as a reed, with a face like a fiddle... What's gone wrong with the great love affair? You know you can tell me. Cry on my shoulder any time. Hey! That's what friends are for.'

'Oh, Amy,' Penny sighed. Amy's tender concern broke the little control she had left, and with her eyes filling with tears she began. 'You were right all along; I'm not cut out to be any man's mistress. You warned me not to move in with Raul but I wouldn't listen. I was so sure we would get married. But now...' she shrugged her slender shoulders dejectedly '...I don't know anything any more. I think he's tired of me. The last night, well...'

She poured out all the events of the past few weeks, all her hopes and fears. She held nothing back, and when she had finished, to her astonishment, Amy laughed!

'Honestly, Penny, from what you have said, you have nothing to worry about. Basically you two argued in Dubai and again in Spain—hardly a reason for parting.

Don't forget it was Raul's suggestion you sell this place—and, incidentally, I think I've found a buyer.'

Raul had told Penny to sell her apartment, insisting that she could get a much better return on her capital by investing it, convincing her that she did not need her own place. And, of course, she had agreed, seeing it as another token of his commitment. But now Penny was not so sure. 'Maybe I should hang onto it,' she said bleakly.

'Oh, for God's sake, be positive! Only two days ago Raul told you stay at his London apartment. That doesn't sound like a man who is tired of you—quite the reverse.'

'Do you really think so?' Penny was desperate for any kind of reassurance.

'Look, you say his housekeeper in Spain thinks he will marry you but he has a problem with commitment. The answer is simple. This is a leap year. Instead of worrying yourself to death over what may or may not happen, the next time you see him ask him to marry you.'

'The twenty-ninth of February is long gone. In case it has escaped your attention, we are now into summer,' Penny said drily.

'The whole year is leap year. Do it. Ask the man. What have you got to lose?'

The outrageous suggestion brought a genuine smile to Penny's face, but still she shook her head. 'No, I couldn't; I haven't the nerve.'

'God!' Amy exclaimed, jumping to her feet in irritation. 'You used to be such a confident, ambitious young woman.' She frowned down at her friend slumped on the settee. 'Remember our plans at college? Within one year we were going to open our own chemist shop. We even had the name picked out—Sense and Sensibility, pinched from Jane Austen. The perfect blend of modern medicine alongside homoeopathic cures. You were the sense and I was the sensibility, with my passion for natural medicine.

'It strikes me that since falling in love you have become the opposite—hopelessly over-sensitive to everything Raul does. You're turning into a wimp, girl. Tell me, how long are you going to continue living with the man? One year, two, five? In love but in limbo...'

The truth was hard to hear but Penny knew that her friend was right. In the first flush of love she had re-lished her life of leisure. But over the past few weeks of long hours alone in hotel rooms or at the *hacienda*, the enforced idleness had finally made her begin to question what she was doing. 'In love but in limbo' was very apt. It was exactly how she felt.

'Come on, Penny, don't be a coward. It's the nineties. Women's lib and all that. When Raul arrives propose to him. Otherwise you might drift on for years, worrying yourself to death about his intentions. Is that what you want?'

It wasn't... 'You're right, I know.'

'Hooray, the woman has seen sense at last. Now repair your make-up and let's go to Bertorelli's in Covent Garden to celebrate your forthcoming marriage—' Amy grinned broadly at Penny '—and pig out on Italian food. You look like you could use a good meal.'

Penny chuckled out loud. 'You are impossible, but I adore you.'

The night was a huge success. They stood and watched the buskers in Covent Garden, and laughed at the antics of a silent clown with a cat on his shoulder. They talked and drank their way through a typical Italian meal of pasta followed by Osso Bucco, and forgot about the coffee.

Finally they flagged down a taxi, and tumbled out of it at the entrance to their old apartment decidedly intoxicated and laughing hysterically for no reason they could remember. Amy passed out on the sofa in the living room and Penny, with greatest difficulty, managed to find a blanket and cover her friend before falling asleep fully dressed in her old bedroom. No thought of returning to Raul's apartment entered her head.

The raucous ringing of a bell broke through Penny's hazed mind. What the hell? she thought, and rolled over on her back. 'Oh, my head,' she groaned aloud, looking around the room with some puzzlement until the events of the previous evening penetrated her sleep-fogged brain.

She lay where she was, trying to gather the energy to get up. At least the ringing had stopped, she thought gratefully, then winced as the sound of a door opening and closing ricocheted through her head like a rifle shot. She closed her eyes and was on the brink of dozing off again when a cheerful voice shouted, 'Coffee, sleepyhead.'

Penny opened her eyes to see Amy, fully dressed in a smart grey suit, grinning down at her. 'What time is it?' she murmured, sitting up. She accepted the mug of coffee from Amy's hand, took a large gulp of the steaming brew, and felt it hit her stomach like a lead balloon.,

'Eight; unlike you, I have to be at work for nine. How do you feel?'

'I'll ring you tomorrow and tell you. It will take me that long to recover.'

'Rubbish. Now I've got to dash, but you take your time and give me a call tonight if you're free. But, if

Raul arrives, don't forget what you decided last night.
Positive action, confidence—ask the man. If he is half
the man you say he is, I'll take a bet that all this pining
and heart-searching will be over.'

Amy made it all seem so simple, Penny thought, and
smiled at her friend. 'Don't worry; you have convinced
me. I'm going to propose to Raul at the first oppor-
tunity. Satisfied?'

'Now, that is the Penny I know and love,' Amy responded, with a wicked grin. 'And don't forget I am
number-one choice for bridesmaid.'

The smile left Penny's face as soon as Amy left the
room. Putting the almost full mug of coffee down on
the bedside table, she swung her feet to the floor and
made straight for the bathroom. She was going to take
Amy's advice, but for her own reasons...

Penny sighed as she shut off the water and stepped out
of the shower onto the mat. She had no idea if Raul had
called last night, and Mrs Grimble's disapproving look
when Penny had arrived back at the apartment at one
in the afternoon had not been reassuring. The older
woman had already seen that none of the beds in the
penthouse apartment had been slept in.

Still, Raul would no doubt call tonight, and, consoling herself with that thought, she dried and dressed
casually in blue jeans and a soft cream cashmere sweater,
then headed for the kitchen and something to eat.

After a light meal—a plain omelette and salad—she
strolled back into the vast living area. One wall was
completely covered by a large bookcase. She ran her hand
along a shelf and picked out the latest Jeffrey Archer
and settled down on the soft green velvet sofa posi-
tioned along one side of the fireplace, and, curving her

bare feet beneath her, began to read. Moments later the
late night took its toll and she was fast asleep.

'Where the hell have you been?'

Penny's eyes flew open in shock; a large male hand
was shaking her shoulder and the words only dimly penetrated her sleep-hazed mind. The book fell from her
hand and she struggled up from her reclining position.

'Raul, you're here,' she murmured softly, the beginnings of a smile pulling the corners of her wide mouth.
It was so good to see him again...

'Pity you could not say the same last night.'

She looked up, wide awake now. 'Raul!' And it
dawned on her that he was nowhere near as happy to
see her as she was him, and her smile died.

He leaned against the arm of the sofa, a dark, un-
smiling figure, his formal clothes oddly dishevelled—his
white shirt open at the neck, his black striped tie pulled
askew.

'Don't bother to deny it, Penny,' he said, his voice
bitingly sardonic. 'I called you every hour from midnight onwards.'

So that was what was bothering him; she gave an
inward sigh of relief. 'I can explain.' She slipped her feet
to the floor and briefly glanced down at where her book
lay on the carpet.

Raul bent down, his long-fingered hands picking it
up. '*Twelve Red Herrings*' he drawled. 'How appropriate; been looking for an excuse, hmm?'

He straightened and thrust his hands into his trouser
pockets, squaring his shoulders. 'If you want to leave
me, you only have to say so.' He sounded coldly remote,
as though he didn't care a jot either way. 'I have no hold
over you, but I would appreciate being informed of your

movements, instead of wasting my precious time chasing over half of Europe to find out where you are.'

She flushed deeply. *His* precious time? How like Raul. His arrogance never ceased to amaze her, and right now it was making her madder than hell. She had agonised for days over the man, and he had the gall to stand in front of her and casually tell her that she could leave him. She could have thumped him.

'Sorry,' she drawled sarcastically. 'I wasn't aware I was supposed to check in every night. As it happened, I spent the evening with Amy,' she began to explain, but didn't get the chance to continue.

'All night, Penny? What do you take me for? A complete fool? I found you laying here asleep in the middle of the afternoon.'

'We—'

'Was he a good lover?' he snarled furiously, his hands falling to her shoulders, and, gripping tightly, he hauled her unceremoniously to her feet. 'Did he make you whimper and cry out as I do?' he demanded, his fingers biting into her skin, the venom in his expression frightening in its intensity. 'Did you whisper the same sweet lying words of love to him as you did to me?'

'No, Raul...' she denied, stricken by the force of his rage. 'You must know—'

'Know what? That you look flushed and exhausted, exactly as you do after making love all night? You forget I'm the one that taught you all you know. I can read the signs on your lying, lovely face; I've put them there so many times myself.'

'You bastard,' she hissed, her face scarlet; she had never, ever spoken to him like that before in their relationship but the injustice of his accusation made her see red.

'I spent the night with Amy because I was too drunk to come home, and I was too drunk because I was drowning my sorrows over you.' She stared at him, her eyes wild in her flushed face. 'And you know why? Because you treat me like some mindless bimbo with no will of my own.' A harsh laugh escaped her. 'Amy was—'

'Amy. I might have known,' he said tightly. 'She has never liked me. I suppose it was her idea for you to stay out all night?'

'We were home by eleven—hardly all night,' she spat back.

Raul stared into her flashing blue eyes. 'Why you listen to that woman I will never know.' He shook his dark head, as though to dispel some unpleasant thought.

The rage draining out of him, he raised a hand from her shoulder and closed his eyes for a second, nipping the bridge of his nose with finger and thumb before adding, 'I'm tired. I'm sorry. I believe you and forgive you.' His deep voice thickened and he stroked a long finger down her smooth cheek, his eyes lingering on her slightly parted lips with sensual anticipation.

She tried to speak but her breath caught in her throat. Her heart was thudding in her breast and suddenly she felt sick. As quickly as his anger had come it had vanished, but she could not hide her hurt so easily.

'Just never give me a shock like that again,' Raul husked. His hand gentled on her shoulders and slid down to curve around her waist; his eyes deepened to a slumbrous, sexy black and his dark head bent to kiss her.

Penny was incredulous and furious. She looked up into his face, at the five o'clock shadow on his hard jaw, and wondered if she had ever known him. She jerked away from him, catching him by surprise.

'That's it, is it? You forgive me, after branding me little better than a whore,' she derided. 'Well, thank you, Raul; you have such faith in me I am quite over-whelmed. Maybe I should kneel at your feet and pay homage to your magnanimity.'

'Hush, Penny.' He held out his hand. 'Come on, it was a genuine mistake; I was worried about you.'

She looked at his outstretched hand and up into his handsome face, and out of nowhere came the thought, How worried? Worried enough to marry her? Amy's idea suddenly didn't seem quite so outrageous. She could put her hand in his and in minutes they would be in bed together. She wanted to but she wanted a whole lot more! She deserved a whole lot more! she thought suddenly, seeing an image of the future, with herself as Raul's sex slave and not much else.

Raul stepped closer, one large hand tilting her chin. 'No more argument, Penny. I was wrong and I'm sorry; put it down to pure male frustration. I've missed you, *querida*.'

Her heart said yes and she raised her hands to his chest, but her head said something else.

She ran her hands up and down his shirt-front, feeling the hard-packed muscle beneath with delight, but as she swayed towards him she hesitated. 'Do you know what year it is, Raul?'

'Around you I hardly know what day it is. You have this shocking effect on me,' he teased softly, and, catching one of her small hands in his, he trailed it down his muscular thigh.

She swallowed a lump in her throat, her heart pounding beneath her breastbone as her fingers touched the hard, aroused length of him beneath the fine wool of his trousers. He wanted her, she knew, and—dear heaven!—she wanted him, but...

'It's leap year, Raul. Will you marry me?' she got out in a breathless rush. Tilting her head back, she stared up at him, her wide blue eyes sparkling with love and hope while her small hands nervously caressed his familiar solid form. A second later she was pushed backwards onto the sofa with a resounding thump, all the air whooshing out of her lungs in a rush.

She didn't know what had hit her, but, glancing up into Raul's furious face, she had a good idea. 'Hardly the response I expected,' she gulped. 'Unless, of course, you intend to join me on the sofa.' She tried to joke, but inside she was filled with a deepening dread.

'Now I get it,' he laughed mirthlessly. 'The arguments of the last few weeks, the defiance, and then the grand finale—staying out all night. What kind of fool do you take me for, Penny?'

'No, Raul.' She wished with all her heart that she had kept her mouth shut, and, pulling herself up to a sitting position, her blue eyes fixed on his rugged face, she lifted a tentative hand to touch his thigh.

He glanced down at her, one dark brow lifted in cynical amusement, before he casually knocked her hand from his leg and stepped back. 'Did you really think depriving me of your sexy body on our last night in Spain and then trying to make me jealous would work?' he drawled mockingly. 'Better women than you have tried to manipulate me into marriage and failed. You're good, but you're not that good, Penny.'

His comment was like a knife in her heart. She wanted to curl up with the pain but she didn't; her pride would not let her. For a long, tense moment she simply stared at him. His black hair was dishevelled and falling over his broad brow, his dark eyes were stony, as was the stubborn jut of his jaw. She let her gaze roam over him—the tanned column of his throat, the broad chest and lean hips. He was standing, feet apart, hands stuck in his trouser pockets, all virile, powerful male.

'I take it that was a no,' she got out between clenched teeth. And, rising to her feet, she would have brushed past him, but he stopped her, a hand on her arm.

'Correct, honey. If and when I take a wife, I will do the asking. No little girl will trap me into marriage. I am far too old to be caught that easy,' he said icily.

Penny wanted to lie down and die, but anger came to her aid. For months she had loved this man, given him everything, loved him unconditionally, because in her foolish heart she had thought he felt the same. What a naïve idiot she was, she thought bitterly. What had he said? She was good, but not that good.

'You're right of course; you are *too* old; I should have realised sooner,' she retaliated, hoping to hurt him just a fraction of how much he had hurt her. She felt his fingers tighten angrily on her arm.

'Nice try, Penny, but insulting me will not make me change my mind,' he gritted.

'Take your hand off me,' she said flatly, her glance resting on the large, strong hand wrapped around her arm. And for the first time since meeting Raul his touch had no effect on her.

'The hands-off policy is hardly going to persuade me to marry you,' Raul laughed harshly, and, spinning her around, held her hard against his strong body. 'And I know you, *querida*; you can't say no.' Bending his head, he feathered his lips across hers.

She trembled helplessly, long before the fiery heat of his mouth melded passionately with her own. She wanted to be immune but she had not the strength to deny him. It was the heaven she longed for but it was also the hell of complete humiliation.

He played her like a violin. His hand roamed her slender form with a sophisticated expertise against which she had no defence. His hard thighs pressed against her soft curves, moving rhythmically, stating his male dominance, forcing her to accept his sensual superiority. She shivered violently, yet she felt as if fire, not blood flowed through her veins.

With a husky laugh Raul set her free and stepped back, his smile mocking her pathetic capitulation to his assault on her senses. 'Forget trying to manipulate me, Penny. You will never win; your body gives you away every time,' he drawled with silky emphasis, his glittering eyes deliberately lowering to her breasts, where her nipples were outlined betrayingly against the soft wool of her sweater, before returning triumphantly to her flushed face.

Penny had never raised a hand to anyone in her life before. But, seeing the smug triumph in his dark eyes, the arrogant stance of his long body, she lost control completely. All the pain and humiliation flooded her brain and, without thought, she lifted her hand and smacked him hard across his self-satisfied face.

'Forget? I intend to forget,' she spat at him, her blue eyes flashing, hating him. 'Forget I ever met you.' She noticed the look of stunned shock in his dark eyes and wanted to laugh, but she didn't get the chance.

Raul's face flushed with violent rage. 'You bitch!' he snarled, and, clamping her to him, he ground his mouth down on hers in a bitter travesty of a kiss.

He plundered her mouth like a man possessed. She felt no pleasure, just dull acceptance, and when he finally pushed her away from him she swayed unsteadily, lifting a trembling hand to brush her swollen lips.

'You asked for that,' Raul said harshly. 'You deliberately provoked me, Penny, but it will not work. If you want to go, *go* . . .'

'Go,' he had said—this from the man who a few short weeks ago in Dubai, after a tumultuous coupling, had sworn that he adored her and that she could ask anything of him and he would give it to her. Lies. All lies . . .

She watched him in bitter, hostile silence for a moment. He had withdrawn behind a cold mask of indifference, his dark eyes blank, expressionless. She had her answer. Raul did not love her. Never had . . .

'I think that will be best,' she said in a cold, dead voice, and, slowly turning away, she added, 'I'm going to pack.'

'Wait, Penny.'

She turned, a brief flicker of hope in her heart. She searched his hard face for some sign of regret. But there was nothing.

'Don't forget this.' Raul withdrew from his pocket a glittering bracelet. 'I found it in the bedroom of our hotel in Dubai after you had left. I was waiting for you to realise you had lost it but obviously you were not impressed by the gift.'

She automatically reached out her hand and took it, slipping it on her wrist. Ashamed to admit that she had forgotten all about her birthday present, she glanced at Raul and imagined that she saw a flash of something like pain in his eyes. The next second she knew that she was mistaken as he added with biting cynicism, 'But it is rather valuable, and under the circumstances I think you have earned it.'

She didn't speak; she couldn't. The world had caved in on her. She loved Raul, and yet he could treat her like some gold-digging tramp he had picked up off the street!

'Nothing to say?' he queried coldly, and, when she still didn't speak, he added with cruel mockery, 'Or perhaps you think you're worth more? So send me a bill, honey, and I'll think about paying.'

The tears she had held at bay for so long threatened to overwhelm her and, spinning on her heel, she dashed out of the room.

Hardly aware of her surroundings, tears blinding her, Penny packed quickly, deliberately leaving behind all the designer clothes that Raul had insisted on buying for her. She checked her purse—she had money enough for a taxi. The glint of metal caught her eyes and she withdrew the plain latch key, then snapped her purse shut.

With a thumping headache to go with her broken heart, suitcase in hand, she walked stiff-backed through the living area. Raul was nowhere in sight. She dropped the key on the hall table and closed the door quietly behind her. She rang for the elevator, and when it arrived, her eyes dry, her face rigid with resolve, she stepped in.

Out on the street she hailed a taxi and gave the driver her own address. The cab pulled away; Penny closed her eyes and never looked back. It was over...

CHAPTER FIVE

'Now, Miss Gold, don't get upset—' the man in the dark blue uniform spoke slowly, softly '—but we have to ask you these questions.'

'Upset!' Penny bawled, tears rolling helplessly down her cheeks. 'Can't you understand someone has stolen my baby, my James?'

It was a nightmare, Penny knew. In a moment she would wake up and everything would be back to normal. She looked up at the plain round clock on the stark white wall. Six o'clock—time to lock up the shop and go upstairs to the apartment and James.

'What about the father, Miss Gold?' a voice said, then louder, 'Miss Gold! The father?'

She stared blindly at the man opposite, his voice seemed to be coming from a long way off.

'Nine times out of ten in this kind of case we find the father has arranged to steal the child.'

Penny could block out reality no longer. The full horror of the situation hit her in every minute, tragic detail... Her head spun and her stomach churned with nausea. She wasn't in the store, James was not upstairs in their apartment with Amy... She was in the medical centre. It was *not* a nightmare. She was *not* going to wake up...

Penny rubbed a shaking hand across her eyes. Someone had stolen her child—the child of her heart, her reason for living. She did not want to believe but there was no escape. James was gone...

'He does not have a father,' she whispered, choking down on her tears.

'Maybe not now, but he must have had one originally. Perhaps the man has decided—'

'No. No, you don't understand,' she cut in. 'The man does not even know my child exists—never has done. Please don't waste any more time. James is only sixteen months old; he is helpless; he needs me,' she pleaded desperately. 'Can't we go and look for him?' Jumping to her feet, she rushed to the door. 'I must; I've got to find him.'

The man in uniform nodded quietly to the doctor and seconds later Penny was being led back to the chair by a man in a white coat.

'I could give you a sedative, Miss Gold,' the doctor said quietly, 'but first we need all the information you can possibly give us. You understand?'

Penny understood; she understood too much. The doctor was protecting his hospital. She had arrived at five for the last appointment of the day, for James to have his triple vaccination at the splendid new health clinic attached to the hospital on the outskirts of Truro.

Penny and James had been the only two in the waiting room when a nurse had walked in and quite reasonably suggested that she take James next door to be weighed and measured before going in to see the doctor for the vaccination. With hindsight Penny knew that she should have queried the nurse's command, but, after working in the store most of the day then driving over to the clinic, leafing through old magazines and keeping James amused with the toys available while they'd waited to see the doctor, she had not been thinking too clearly and had handed James over, with the nurse's helpful instructions ringing in her ears.

'Collect up your things and go through to the treatment room. It won't take a minute, and we'll join you.'

Penny had sat for what had seemed an awfully long time, getting more and more agitated, with no sign of the nurse or James. Finally she'd jumped up, determined to go and find out what was causing the delay, when Dr Brown had entered with the words 'Sorry for the delay, Miss Gold. Now, where is the little chap?'

The next half-hour had been like a horror movie, with Penny playing the victim's role.

Now she choked back a sob and looked once more at the faces around her—the blond blue-eyed Dr Brown, a chief administrator and three policemen—two in plain clothes. It was a large surgery, very new, very white. She closed her eyes and shook her head.

It was ironic; not so many years ago when her own father had been a GP he'd visited children in their homes to give them a vaccination, and he'd always given them ten pence for being good. The memory brought fresh tears to her eyes. Now, with rationalisation, the small town of Royal Harton, where Amy and Penny had set up their store, Sense and Sensibility, two years ago, no longer had its own GP but shared a medical practice with a half-dozen other villages in Cornwall.

'So we can eliminate the father?' a deep voice asked.

Eliminate him! Exterminate him! She didn't give a fig! 'Yes, yes, yes,' she answered hysterically. She had eliminated Raul from her life years ago when she had left his apartment and never looked back. She had never seen or spoken to him since. James was the only person she cared about; he would be crying, terrified, with a strange woman in strange surroundings. 'Please, just do something. Damn you! Do something.'

There was a commotion outside in the hall, but Penny was not aware of it, too overwhelmed by her own misery and guilt to register clearly what was going on around her. It was only when Amy's comforting arm slid around her slender shoulders and Penny looked up into her friend's compassionate face that she managed to claw back some semblance of self-control.

'Oh, Amy...' she whispered. 'My baby—someone has stolen James and it is all my fault.' And another paroxysm of weeping enveloped her.

'Hush, hush. Don't blame yourself; it wasn't your fault. If you want to blame anyone, blame me. If only I hadn't insisted on taking most of the day off to visit Nick in St Austell you wouldn't have needed to wait till the last appointment and none of this would have happened.'

'No!' Penny could not let her friend take the blame. If it had not been for Amy sharing the running of the shop and the care of James, Penny would never have been able to start a business and keep her baby with her. Thinking 'if only' never helped anyone; life had taught Penny that much. Bravely she straightened her shoulders and, clasping Amy's free hand for comfort, looked straight at the policeman.

'Sorry. Please ask me anything—anything you like.' She swallowed hard to free the lump in her throat. 'Just so long as I get my son back...'

And so began the worst, the most horrific, traumatic twenty-four hours of her life...

If she had thought it hard to get over Raul, it was as nothing to the anguish, the soul destroying despair of having her son stolen from her.

*   *   *

'Please, Penny, take the sleeping tablets the doctor prescribed and go to bed,' Amy begged, her worried gaze following the pacing figure of her friend. 'It's after midnight. I will stay up all night and take any calls. You need your sleep. You need to be fresh and alert when they bring James back.'

It had taken all Amy's considerable powers of persuasion simply to get Penny back to the apartment above the chemist, but she was not prepared to give up yet. It broke her heart to see her friend so distraught. As for James, her much loved godson, she didn't dare think about him; she had to be strong for Penny's sake.

'They will get him back, Penny; believe me, they will. You know me; I've always been a bit psychic; I know these things. So please try to get some rest. James will need you in the morning.'

'Do you think so? Do you really think so?' Penny demanded hoarsely, her throat dry from weeping. She was grasping at straws but she was desperate for even the faintest reassurance.

'Yes, I am certain,' Amy said adamantly.

'Perhaps I will lie down for a few minutes.' And with a bleak, watery attempt at a smile Penny wandered down the hall to her bedroom. But her feet stopped outside a different door, and slowly, fearfully, she pushed it open and walked in. In some far corner of her stunned mind she hoped against hope to see James...

She stared at the Victorian-style cot, saw the outline of a form and willed it to be James. She crossed the room and leaned over the side of the crib, her shaking hand reaching out and clutching the small arm. She felt the soft hair and she could not fool herself for a second longer.

Clasping the teddy bear to her breast, she dropped her head, and the tears rolled silently down her cheeks while her shoulders shook with her anguish. Her legs refused to support her and she fell to her knees on the floor, long, shuddering convulsions racking her slender frame.

'Why? Oh, Lord, why? Why my child?' And she began to pray fervently over and over again, 'Please, please, Lord, give me back my son.'

She didn't hear or see Amy stop at the door, shake her head and walk away again. She heard nothing except the scream of anguish in her soul mingling with the pitiful memory of her baby's cry.

Daylight came, and with it the arrival of the plain-clothes policemen again. The early-morning news carried the story of the missing child and reporters from all the major national and even international newspapers appeared, milling around in the street outside the shop and apartment. The phone didn't stop ringing until Amy simply unplugged it. Finally a camera crew arrived, with a female presenter from the BBC.

Penny, numb with shock and desperate, agreed to everything and anything. All she wanted was her child back. An appeal and interview with the distraught mother on the one o'clock news might just do the trick. Someone somewhere might see it and recognise the photograph of James and know where he was. Or even the kidnapper might see the broadcast and, recognising the extent of Penny's suffering, restore the child unharmed. Anything was possible!

The tall dark man glanced uninterestedly around the familiar room and headed straight for the bar. Dropping a black hide briefcase on the floor, he poured himself a large whisky and, glass in hand, crossed to the sofa and collapsed on it.

He took a long swallow of the amber liquid and, with his other hand, idly picked up the television remote control from the sofa table and pressed it on. He watched the flickering images on the screen without really paying much attention, tired from the early-morning flight from Spain.

Suddenly he jerked upright, instantly alert, his hand increasing the volume on the television. The announcer had mentioned the name Penelope Gold... He saw a picture of a chubby, dark, curly-haired, brown-eyed baby boy, sitting on his mother's knee and laughing up at the beautiful, flaxen-haired woman. He drained the whisky in one swallow, his hand tightening involuntarily around the glass as the voice continued.

'The abduction of James, a sixteen-month-old baby boy, from a Cornish medical centre yesterday afternoon has shocked the whole nation. The police have issued the following identikit picture of the bogus nurse thought responsible for the kidnapping, in the hope that someone somewhere might have seen or have information that will lead to the return of Baby James to his distraught mother.

'There will now follow a short interview and a personal appeal for the baby's return by Miss Penelope Gold, the mother of Baby James.'

The female interviewer was all sympathy. 'I believe, Penelope, you are an orphan and a single parent. James is the only family you have. Is that correct?'

'Yes, James is everything to me, and I beg whoever has taken him to please, please be kind to him and please give him back to me. We have never been apart for a single night since he was born. Please, I beg whoever has taken him, whatever agony you have suffered to make you do something like this, please give James back. He is my life.'

The panic, the pain in the woman's impassioned plea was heart-wrenching, and to the shocked horror of the man watching the television the interviewer took full advantage of her distress.

'I know it's hard for you, Penelope, but I have to ask you this. Statistically, the police say, in most such cases the father is behind the kidnapping. Can you be absolutely sure that does not apply with James?'

'James does not have a father; he only has me...' And with rising hysteria evident in her voice she continued, 'He never had a father.' She was shivering, her arms folded defensively over her chest, lost in misery and fear for her child. 'No, no, no, there is no father, I tell you. Only me. A woman stole my baby, my James...' And the recording ended with a small, ginger-haired woman walking into shot and putting her arm around the sobbing Penelope Gold.

The image on the screen vanished as the man clenched his hands. The sound of shattering glass echoed in the sudden silence of the room. The man didn't notice the blood oozing between his fingers. He was numb, frozen in disbelief...

A long while later he rose to his feet and crossed to the telephone. A casual observer would have seen that his saturnine features were set in an impenetrable mask, betraying not a flicker of emotion as he dialled a number and cancelled his appointments for the next few days. But, to a more discerning observer, looking into the dark eyes would have been like looking into the depths of hell itself. The red-hot fury, the monumental rage, was impossible to disguise.

*   *   *

'Penny. Penny.'

Someone was shaking her shoulder; she tried to open her eyes but they felt as if they were glued shut.

'James—they've found him.'

She heard the voice through a drug-induced daze, but at the mention of her son's name she battled through muffled layers of consciousness and finally opened her eyes. Amy was at the bedside, her small face lit up like a Christmas tree, her red hair standing out as though she had had an electric shock.

'Did you hear me, Penny? That was the police on the phone. James is safe...'

Penny dragged herself up the bed, great big tears rolling silently down her hollow cheeks. 'James—they've found him.' Her heart expanded in her chest till she thought it would burst; she grabbed Amy's hand.

'Where? Where is he? Is he well? You're sure?' The words tumbled out as she forced her legs over the side of the bed and tried to stand. She silently cursed the doctor who, after her breakdown during the television interview, had given her an injection that had knocked her out. She shook her head to try and clear her mind. 'Please, Amy, where is he? I must go to him.' And, struggling to her feet, she swayed slightly.

'Steady, pet,' Amy said, grinning from ear to ear, and placing an arm around Penny's waist, she led her towards the bathroom, talking all the time.

'Your television appearance did the trick. Apparently the woman who took James did it on the spur of the moment. She actually was a nurse, but not at that hospital. Tragically her child died of leukaemia three months ago in the same hospital.

'She was wandering around, simply because it was the last place she had seen her child alive, when she saw you and James.

'Her husband works night-shifts and knew nothing about it. On returning from work this morning he went straight to bed. He got up at lunchtime and turned on the television to watch the news, and then strolled into the kitchen, expecting his wife to be at work. Instead he found her in the kitchen with James. He immediately rang the police.'

'Oh, Amy.' Penny turned into her friend's arms and and they hugged each other for a long moment, too overcome with emotion to speak but both crying tears of joy.

'One more shot, please, Penny,' a dozen different voices shouted.

Penny was too happy to argue. Hugging James in her arms, her smile as wide as the Pacific Ocean, she posed for the assembled photographers, her eyes glistening with tears of joy and relief.

'It's all right, baby,' she murmured, nuzzling the dark, silky curls on her son's head, and he responded by chortling and grabbing her loosely pinned hair in a tiny fist. Pulling hard, he dislodged the pale silk mass which fell around her shoulders.

Penny laughed out loud with delight and, squeezing James to her breast, said, 'Thank you,' to the reporters and turned to go back into the shop. An involuntary shiver shuddered through her and she hesitated at the door, glancing warily back over her shoulder.

But James had caught sight of Amy in the store and wriggled to be put down, saying, 'Auntie Amy.' So Penny did not notice the long black Jaguar parked on the opposite side of the village square, or the stony-faced man sitting behind the wheel. If she had she might not have dismissed her flash of foreboding as nothing more than someone walking over her grave.

'I want to pinch myself, I'm so happy,' Penny said later that night as she stood beside James's cot and watched him sleep.

'I know, Penny,' Amy said quietly. 'But don't you think you should leave him to sleep now? You haven't let him out of your sight since the policewoman brought him back. You've moved his cot into your bedroom. I can understand how you feel, but I'm not sure it's such a good idea. You are going to have to leave him, some time.'

Penny turned. 'It's all right, Amy, I know. Only just not yet, hmm?'

'Come on into the kitchen and I'll make you a cup of my superior hot chocolate and marshmallow—sinfully fattening but guaranteed to please...'

'Oh, my! An offer I can't refuse,' Penny chuckled, and, bending to press one more kiss on her son's brow, she followed Amy out of the bedroom.

Three hours later Penny lay curled up on her side in bed, her eyes fixed on the sleeping child barely a foot away in his cot. She was bone-tired after the trauma of the past twenty-four hours, but sleep was elusive.

She knew that James was fine; he had been thoroughly checked by the police doctor and Dr Brown. In fact he did not seem to have been affected at all by his experience. He had called the woman who'd kidnapped him 'Auntie' and had apparently played with dozens of toys.

Penny knew that she should be grateful that the woman had looked after him so well, and she had told the police that she did not want to press charges. Unfortunately it was not up to her. The Crown Prosecution Service insisted that the woman had to be charged but had said she would be treated leniently—probably made to take psychiatric help, which Penny knew would be for the woman's own good.

The reason for her sleeplessness was much more complex. It could have turned out much worse. She could have lost James for good; he could have died. The abduction of James had made her question her own mortality, and made her face up to the fact that, if anything— God forbid!—happened to her, her child would be alone in the world.

She had, after long months of anguish, managed to come to terms with Raul's rejection. He had never loved her; he had callously used her, nothing more... With James's birth she had dismissed any notion of telling Raul. James was her much loved baby and she alone was responsible for him. But now the past came back to haunt her, and she was no longer so sure that she had done the right thing.

She remembered the last humiliating meeting with Raul and walking out, but the next few weeks she had lived in a feverish whirl, determined to forget him.

The very next week Penny had sold her apartment to the buyer Amy had mentioned. The man worked for the National Geographic Society and had spent the past three years on a research and survey expedition in the Antarctic. Penny had simply wanted to get out of the city where she had suffered her worst humiliation. It had all worked out rather well.

She and Amy had spent the following weekend in Cornwall, attending Mike and Tanya's wedding in Tanya's home town of Helston. They had driven through the picturesque town of Royal Harton and noticed the 'For Sale' sign on an empty pharmacy in the market square. Old stone and quaint, it was the ideal place to launch Sense and Sensibility. On the way back from the wedding they had enquired about the business, and within another couple of weeks had bought it. Then they'd moved in.

Penny stirred restlessly on the bed. It had all seemed so perfect; she had admitted her fear to Amy that she might be pregnant and Amy had been wonderful about it. Being strictly honest, Penny had already suspected that she was pregnant when she had proposed to Raul. Otherwise she would never have done it. She knew the exact night her beloved son had been conceived—the only time Raul had lost control, the night of their first argument, in Dubai.

She glanced at the sleeping child, her heart full of love, and something more—something she did not want to recognise. Guilt. Regret, maybe. In the light of the past twenty-four hours, she was forced to question her right to deprive James of his father... Still—she yawned widely, her eyelids drooping—her son was safe and there was no hurry to decide one way or another.

But in that she was wrong...

'I'll open the shop this morning,' Amy said as the three of them sat around the small breakfast table in the cheerful pine kitchen. James, in his high chair, was shovelling mashed banana and cereal in his mouth with chubby fingers, the spoon lying neglected by his Beatrix Potter bowl.

Penny smiled at his antics and agreed. 'If you don't mind.'

'My pleasure, Penny; you spend the day with James. After all, I'm hardly likely to be inundated with prescriptions.'

'That's true.' Penny frowned.

'Cheer up. We will be fine, and Doris is coming in as usual so you have nothing to worry about.'

Doris was their one full-time employee—a young local girl and an absolute gem. She had a gift for picking stock that would appeal to the tourists—a godsend since the new medical centre had opened with its own pharmacy attached and had taken a lot of their trade. The prescription side of the business had halved in the past few months and really no longer warranted two pharmacists.

But, luckily for Sense and Sensibility, from Easter to October the tourists flocked to Cornwall, outnumbering the residents about a hundred to one, so the profit margin had not dropped too much. But it was still a worry.

Penny spent a hectic morning with James; the first post delivered hundreds of letters of sympathy and support along with a host of toys, mostly cuddly. The apartment had a separate front door from the shop and the doorbell seemed to ring every five minutes with another gift from a well-wisher. Penny was overwhelmed by the generosity of complete strangers and was rapidly getting worn out running up and down the stairs to answer the door.

Grasping James firmly around the middle and pinning him to her hip, she raced downstairs yet again. James thought it was a huge joke and that all his birthdays had come at once. Penny was not so sure. But when she opened the door she had to laugh.

One of the BBC cameramen of the day before was standing with the most enormous cuddly panda in his arms. Apparently the whole crew had had a whip round and bought it for James. Thanking him profusely, and brushing the happy tears from her eyes, she struggled back upstairs, trailing the enormous panda and James.

Luckily, by the time James was ready for his lunch and afternoon nap, the callers had tailed off. Washed and fed, and with a cot overflowing with toys, James blew bubbles up at her as she leaned over his cot and pressed a swift kiss on his cherubic face. 'I love you, baby,' she murmured, and was rewarded with a beatific if sleepy smile.

'Love Mamma,' James said happily.

It never ceased to amaze Penny how clever her son was. He had said his first word at nine months and now almost spoke in sentences. Puffed up with maternal pride, she watched him until he slept, and then reluctantly left the bedroom and walked down the hall to the living room.

She had a mountain of work to do—washing, cleaning—but instead she flopped on the prettily covered chintz sofa, and, curling her bare feet up beneath her, pulled the ribbon from her pony-tail and shook her head, running her fingers through her long hair before sinking back against the soft cushion.

Penny could hardly believe that it was all over. James was safe. And with a deep sigh of relief she closed her eyes and said another silent prayer of gratitude.

Her eyes flew open at the sound of the doorbell yet again. She was off the sofa and down the stairs like a shot. James had just gone to sleep. No way did she want him awake again so quickly.

She flung open the door. Pushing her tangled hair off
her face, she said, 'Please, you'll wake the baby.' A large
figure of a man was blocking the doorway. 'Can I help
y—?' And it was then that she raised her eyes to the
stranger's face and gasped on the 'you'. Penny froze in
astonishment, the colour draining from her cheeks.

'Aren't you going to ask me in?' Raul drawled. Ignoring her gasp of shock at his appearance, he did not
wait for an answer but simply brushed past her, closing
the door behind him.

'Wait a minute,' Penny spluttered.

'I think not, Penelope. I have waited too long already.
Over two years too long, it would seem, and what I have
to say to you would be best said in private.'

In the close confines of the narrow hall his presence
was overpowering. She shuddered and looked away from
his too-penetrating gaze, but the rest of him only served
to remind her what a truly awesome specimen of the
male sex he was.

A black leather blousonjacket accentuated the width
of his broad shoulders, and the close-fitting cinnamon-
coloured knit shirt was open at the neck, blending with
the strong, tanned throat. Long legs were encased in
black jeans of an indecently hip-hugging fit. She dropped
her head and stared at his shoes. Gucci loafers, of course!
What else?

She closed her eyes, an agonising surge of bitter resentment rocketing through her. The man with everything but a heart, she thought, her hatred of his kind
tightening her mouth in disgust. Pull yourself together,
she told herself sternly, and, taking a deep, calming
breath, opened her eyes. He is only a man, and not a
very nice one at that...

Lifting her head, she coldly faced him. 'I have nothing whatsoever to say to you.' Refusing to be cowed by his glittering, remorseless gaze, which seemed to see right through her, she reached out and curled her hand around the doorhandle. 'Leave. Now,' she said curtly, but instead a large hand covered hers and the door remained firmly closed.

'No one orders me to leave, and certainly not a devious, conniving little—'

'And I will not be insulted in my own home,' she cut in. His touch was like a searing brand on her flesh. She tore herself free, clutching her two hands together convulsively, determined to deny the instant effect that his lightest touch had evoked. His dark eyes blazed with fury and he muttered something under his breath that she did not catch, and she did not care.

'I trust I have made myself clear. Please leave.' She knew in her bones that she had little or no hope of forcing Raul to go, but it had to be worth a try. This man had destroyed her once, torn her apart, humiliated her completely. It had taken her years to recover, to regain her pride and self-respect. But never again, she vowed.

Raul's narrowed gaze rested on her standing defiantly before him and then sank to her entwined hands, an expression of something very like disgust tautening his hard features.

'That is unfortunately no longer an option,' he said icily. 'Had you told me I had a son earlier, none of the trauma, the horror of the past two days would ever have happened. Think about that, my sweet Penny, when you attempt to defend your behaviour,' he drawled with biting cynicism, turning and striding up the stairs while she stood frozen to the spot.

She watched him reach the top and disappear into her apartment, her heartbeat racing like an express train. But the worst part was the knowledge that the damn man was probably right!

No one in the world would be allowed to steal anything or anyone from Raul Da Silva. No one would dare try. And, with that depressing thought in her mind, she could do nothing but trudge reluctantly up the stairs after him.

CHAPTER SIX

SHE should tear after him and throw him out. Instead Penny was grateful for the few moments alone to try and marshal her thoughts into some kind of order. Raul here, in her home. It was too much to take in. A thousand questions spun in her tired mind. How had he found her? More importantly, why?

After the trauma of the past day or so the last thing she needed was a spectre from the past coming back to haunt her. Raul could not have chosen a worse time to reappear in her life. Her confidence in herself as a mother had taken a severe battering, and she was in no condition to fight with Raul.

A creeping paralysis slowed her steps and she stopped just inside the door of the living room, folding her arms across her chest in a defensive attitude. Raul was standing in the middle of the room—a sinister dark force, totally out of place in her pretty home.

'Nice, but hardly the luxury you were accustomed to,' Raul drawled cynically, his dark gaze sweeping the room and settling on her white face. 'And hardly the money. A country pharmacy-cum-gift shop is not about to make you wealthy.'

His arrogant, sneering condemnation of her work and her lifestyle was the incentive she needed to regain her wits and her temper.

'You've got the wrong person. I was never accustomed to luxury. That was your taste, never mine,' she snapped. 'And, as for the single-minded pursuit of money, it doesn't seem to have done you much good if the grey in your hair is a testament to your wealth.'

Penny did not care if he was insulted. Raul deserved it. She had never wanted his money, only his love, until she'd discovered that he did not know the meaning of the word.

She was proud of what she had achieved and no one could take that away from her. Not even Raul.

She glanced around the familiar room, at the original pine fireplace, lovingly stripped and restored, at the alcoves either side lined with shelves that housed the music centre, television and dozens of books, at the modest, floral-patterned, chintz-covered three-piece suite, the coffee table, the carpet, curtains and wallpaper—all in complementary shades of rose and green. It was her home and she loved it, but with Raul's presence it seemed to shrink in size to the proportions of a doll's house.

'It wasn't money that caused every one of these grey hairs.' She had not realised that he had moved until his hand snaked out and caught her shoulder. 'It was a lying female,' he grated harshly, his dark eyes narrowed furiously on her pale face.

Penny shrugged, trying to dislodge his hold on her and at the same time, she hoped, convey her indifference to him. 'Don't tell me the sweet Dulcie has given you your marching orders again?' she queried sarcastically, privately thinking that it was no more than he deserved.

'This is between you and me and our son. Forget Dulcie,' he advised bitingly. 'You have a hell of a lot more to worry about.'

Penny stared up at him, her blue eyes widening in alarm. His 'our son' struck terror in her heart. Now she knew why he was here. 'I don't think I need to worry,' she muttered, nervously licking her dry lips with the tip of her tongue.

He smiled—a satanic twist of his hard lips. 'But I know so, my sweet Penny. For starters, worry about depriving a man of his son.' A black brow lifted. 'He is mine. Don't bother trying to deny it.'

'No, he is mine,' she shot back, infuriated by his arrogant claim to fatherhood when he had never given a damn before now. 'You were his biological father, nothing more. A test-tube these days fulfils the same function.'

A flash of naked, seething anger ignited the golden flecks in his deep brown eyes. 'I am still his father, even if you did do your damnedest to blacken my name on national television.'

She had not meant to do that, and flushed guiltily. 'I was upset. But it was still the truth,' she retaliated.

'You were upset! How the hell do you think I felt? I arrived at the penthouse yesterday lunchtime, switched on the television and discovered I had a child I knew nothing about—a child, moreover, who had been kidnapped. And there you were, calling me the worst form of low life.'

'I never mentioned your name.'

'You might as well have done. You must have known I would claim my son.'

She ran a nervous hand through the tangle of her long hair. Amazingly it had never once entered her head. Her only thought had been for her lost child. She looked up and caught his grim, implacable glance and went pale. 'It never occurred to me.'

'My God! As naïve as ever. And you actually think you have nothing to worry about. Let me enlighten you, Penny; you have a great deal to worry about unless you do exactly as I say,' he drawled with a silken menace that made her blood run cold. 'Now! Where is he? I want to see him.'

'You can't. He is asleep,' she answered, swallowing hard on the fear that threatened to choke her.

'I can wait.'

She did not doubt it for a second. She tried to think; Raul had seen her on television ... In her distress over James it had never once occurred to her that Raul might be in London and see the appeal. 'You were in England, then?' she voiced her thought out loud.

'Exactly.' His fingers bit painfully into her shoulder, the one word carrying an undeniable threat.

A shiver of fear ran down her spine, making her tremble. 'You're hurting me,' she said in a soft, frightened voice. But the fear was all for James, not herself. No way was Raul taking James. She had lost him once for twenty-four hours; that was enough.

She had not even told Amy the whole truth, but secretly she half blamed Raul for the abduction of her son. If she had not been glancing through *Hello* magazine in the waiting room and just seen a photograph of Raul and Dulcie at some grand gala in Madrid— Dulcie sporting a very ostentatious diamond ring on her engagement finger—Penny might have had enough sense not to hand James over to the bogus nurse.

'You're lucky I don't kill you. That was my first desire,' he informed her, the violence in his tone shocking her rigid, 'until I spoke to my lawyer and realised that at the moment I need you in order to see my son.'

His mention of a lawyer was so icily precise and so like him, Penny thought bitterly. Not for Raul the rush to support and comfort the panic-stricken mother, but a discreet call to his lawyer to prepare his case. He could

not have underlined more clearly how little he thought
of her.

She hated him in that moment with a rage she could
barely contain. She wanted to scream that he was not
getting her son, to claw at his conceited, arrogant face,
but she did not dare. She had to know his intentions if
she was to protect her child. So instead she stood with
head bent and made herself count to twenty under her
breath, fighting to maintain some self-control.

'No comment, Penny, darling?' he prompted scathingly. His other hand reaching to tip her chin up, he
stared down at her deadly pale face, then lower, his gaze
roaming slowly over her in insolent appraisal.

Penny forced herself to suffer his contemptuous
perusal without flinching. She knew what he would see,
and for a second she wished that she had dressed more
conservatively that morning. A skimpy white vest left
her arms bare and her denim cut-offs clung to her slim
hips, leaving her bare-legged and barefoot. Hardly the
power dressing necessary to face a powerful enemy such
as Raul, she thought wryly.

But she refused to let him see how angry and frightened
she was. She hated him, and hell would freeze over before
she let him get anywhere near her precious James. Unfortunately, putting her feelings into words was not so
easy when Raul towered threateningly over her, holding
her. She was still reeling with the shock of his arrival
and silently raging inside that he dared come.

'Brave but foolish,' Raul remarked, seeing the defiance in her blue eyes.

She stared coldly back at him. The first thing she had
noticed when he had pushed his way into her home was
that his thick black hair was liberally sprinkled with grey.
But now she saw the change in his features. His face was

thinner, the cheekbones more pronounced. The lines around his eyes had deepened with the passage of time and two deep lines bracketed his hard mouth.

He was still an incredibly attractive man; his new leanness simply made him appear even more powerful, more predatory, like some sleek black panther waiting to leap... The trick was to make sure that it was not her he leapt on, Penny told herself sternly. Not easy when she was acutely aware of his hand on her shoulder and cupping her chin.

Marshalling her thoughts, she picked her words carefully. 'Not foolish,' she said slowly. 'Age and motherhood have taught me patience and caution. I can spare you five minutes. Say what you have to say and go.' She was rather proud of her response, even though her heart was fluttering like a captive bird, and she silently congratulated herself on her hard-won maturity.

'Caution! You?' Raul laughed—a harsh, humourless sound that grated on the ear. 'You don't know the meaning of the word,' he mocked.

'And you don't know me,' Penny clipped back.

'Oh, but I do. And I can prove it,' he said dangerously.

Penny tensed as his darkening glance caught and held hers. Inexplicably her heart lurched in her breast. She could not break away from the hypnotic power of his glittering eyes. She was like a mouse hypnotised by the hooded gaze of a cobra.

Raul's hand dropped from her chin to her waist and she was firmly locked to the long, hard length of his body. She knew that she should resist but instead she watched, her pulse racing out of control as his head dipped and his mouth fastened over hers, hard, hot and demanding a response.

It had been so long since she had been held by a man, kissed by a man, and the fact that it was Raul, her one and only lover, had an instant effect on her senses. The feelings she had repressed for over two years welled up inside her; she felt dizzy, her mind spinning as sexual need as fierce as it was unexpected set every nerve in her body quivering with frustrated desire.

With an urgent, throaty growl of passion Raul plunged his tongue hungrily, erotically in her mouth. He slid one hand under her vest to glide teasingly up her naked back, his touch on her bare flesh sending shock waves through her slender frame. His other hand curved around her buttocks while a strong thigh urged her legs apart. She felt the powerful thrust of his male arousal and help-lessly arched closer into him. The deep, searing kiss, the heat of his hard body, the scent of him, so achingly fam-iliar, and she was drowning in a sea of sensuous delight.

She tried to fight the urge to fling her arms around him and kiss him back. Her legs trembled, her fists clenched and unclenched but it was no contest. De-feated, she raised her hands to his chest, her fingers lin-gering on the soft fabric of his shirt, lovingly tracing the muscular wall of his chest.

His mouth left hers and Penny gasped for breath. But Raul had no such difficulty. He gazed deep into her passion-glazed eyes. 'You see, Penny? I know you better than you think. Caution is not in your vocabulary when it comes to sex,' he voiced mockingly.

Shame turned her face scarlet and she pulled back, stumbling slightly in her haste to escape. Raul reached out a hand to steady her and she knocked it away.

Furious with Raul but even more furious with herself, she forgot any notion of staying in control, and raged back viciously. 'Sex is all you ever think about, you arrogant pig. Well, I've got news for you. You might be able to turn a woman on for a moment—big deal! So can millions of other men,' she derided. 'But, in the long term, even with all your wealth and power, you are a dead loss. And as for getting your hands on my son forget it; you haven't a cat in hell's chance.'

'The events of the past two days would suggest otherwise,' Raul said with a cynical edge.

Penny stiffened, her anger draining away as ice spread slowly through her body while Raul casually turned aside and shrugged off his jacket, dropping it on the sofa. Equally casually he strode across the room to lean against the fireplace before turning to look back at her and deliver the *coup de grâce*.

'After all, Penny, you were hardly very cautious with the boy, handing him over to a complete stranger,' he opined acidly.

Penny was frozen on the spot. She stared with pain-filled eyes at his hard, ruthless face. Her throat tightened and she had to look away to blink back the tears. There was nothing he could have said that would have hurt her more. 'I won't argue with you,' she said quietly. 'But neither will I let you have my son.'

He shook his dark head and grimaced. 'I have no intention of depriving you of your child.'

She wanted to believe him but she did not trust him an inch. 'So you say,' she muttered.

'Believe it,' Raul said tersely, and, idly picking up a picture frame from the mantelpiece, which held a photograph of James as a baby, he stared at it for a long moment. 'How old was he when this was taken?' he asked in a thick voice.

'Six months.'

'He's beautiful.'

'Yes,' Penny agreed. Actually, he was the living image of his father, and the worried thoughts that had kept her awake last night came back to her. She had almost decided to tell Raul about James. Maybe Raul's turning up today was fate. The decision had been made for her.

A weary sigh escaped her. She glanced sideways at Raul, so large and elegant, leaning casually against the fireplace, and wondered fearfully exactly what he wanted.

'For God's sake, Penny! You're standing there like a frightened rabbit. Sit down before you fall down, and let's talk like two sensible adults.'

She did as he said; she did not have much choice. Perched on the edge of the sofa, it seemed to Penny as if she had an awfully long way to look up at where Raul was standing, a dark, brooding frown marring his handsome face. She waited, expecting him to speak; the silence lengthened, the tension in the air almost tangible until finally she could stand it no longer.

'You said talk,' she reminded him curtly.

Raul replaced the photograph on the mantelpiece and, ignoring her words, began pacing up and down the room. Finally he stopped in front of Penny. 'When will the boy wake up?' he demanded.

She glanced up and caught a glimpse of some emotion she did not recognise in his dark eyes. 'Half an hour, maybe,' she murmured. If she had not known better she could have sworn that Raul was nervous.

'I see.' He ran a hand distractedly through his thick hair and lowered himself down beside her on the sofa. 'Enough time, I suppose.'

'For what?' Penny asked, edging away from the far too masculine thigh brushing her bare leg.

Raul noted her reaction, his mouth quirking in the semblance of a smile. Then he floored her completely. 'To arrange the wedding, of course.'

She was on her feet in a flash and spun round to stare down at him in horror. He couldn't be serious. No. She was jumping to conclusions. Remember, she reprimanded herself sternly, you're a mature adult, a mother, a businesswoman.

'Who is getting married?' she asked, and answered her own question. 'Of course—you and Dulcie.' Suddenly it was very clear, and Penny's temper took off again. 'If you think for one second I would let that woman anywhere near my child, forget it. You can have access rights but that is all.'

'Not Dulcie. You and I, Penny,' Raul corrected her coolly. 'It is obvious the boy needs a father's protection. I've decided marriage is the best solution all round.'

He had decided! Never mind that he already had a fiancée! Raul the magnificent had decided. The master's voice... Penny thought bitterly. 'Not in my lifetime,' she said bluntly.

'You have not given it any thought, Penny. Consider all I can give the boy. Remember years ago you asked me to marry you. Nothing has changed except now I agree.'

'No,' she reiterated, hating to be reminded of her last humiliation at this man's hands. She would never take the risk of that happening again.

'Don't be so damned selfish.' Raul grabbed her wrist and pulled her down beside him on the sofa once again.

'Let go of me.'

'Not until you listen. I am trying to be fair to you, Penny, because you have suffered a terrible experience,' he said earnestly. 'I am trying to keep my temper. But

I have not forgotten that you never once mentioned you were pregnant when you asked me to marry you. If you had I would have agreed and none of the trauma of the past couple of days need ever have happened. The chemistry is still there between us; we can have a good marriage and our son a good family life.'

Penny looked at him long and hard. There was no doubting that he was absolutely serious, and for a second she actually considered what it would be like married to Raul. Sexually he was perfect—every woman's fantasy lover rolled into one. Her heart stopped momentarily and Raul's dark eyes gleamed triumphantly into hers, as if he was reading her mind.

'You know I'm right, Penny.'

It was the superb self-confidence in his tone that infuriated her, and she remembered the rest—his domineering personality, his orders on what to wear and where to go, his workaholic lifestyle, flitting around the world at a moment's notice. He was certainly not cut out to be a father and family man. In fact James would probably see more of his father if Raul had to make an appointment to meet the boy than he ever would living with his dad. And then there was Dulcie!

Suddenly his suggestion struck Penny as ludicrous. 'You're kidding, of course. You, who vowed you would never be trapped into marriage, have the gall to sit in my home and propose marriage to get my child.' A humourless laugh escaped her. 'Sorry, no.'

'Think again, Penny.'

'I don't need to; the answer is no.'

'I could fight you in court for custody.' He said the words casually, with no more inflection than a weatherman reading the forecast.

Penny looked at him in disbelief. He was lounging back on the sofa, apparently at ease. 'You would do that?' she said tightly.

Raul gave her a chilling smile. 'It's an option,' he said, giving nothing away.

His dark eyes blandly met her furious blue but she was too angry to bother trying to hide her hatred and disgust. In fact, she realised, she was not even surprised. From the minute Raul had said 'our son' she had been waiting for something like this. 'You would never win. Not in an English court. Especially after the recent publicity.'

'But can you take that chance, Penny?' he asked brutally. 'I have the time, the wealth and the best lawyers at my disposal, whereas you have very little money or time to fight me.'

True to character. To Raul wealth was everything, Penny thought bitterly, but he was not getting her son. 'Try it,' she challenged him. 'But know I will fight you to the death to keep my son.'

A loud shout of 'mamma' from James stopped whatever acid comment Raul had been about to make.

Penny immediately leapt to her feet, and didn't notice the menacing intent in Raul's expression. 'He's awake.' She stated the obvious to give herself time to think. She knew that she would have to make sure she acted cool and in control around Raul. It was the only way to get through to a man like him, and now was a good time to start. She took a few steps and then turned back to him. He had not moved; it was as if the sound of the child's voice had frozen him on the spot.

'*My* son—' she emphasised the 'my', '—can wait a minute; he has plenty of toys in his cot. But the situation between us cannot.'

Her decision made, she proceeded coldly. 'Do you remember your final words to me years ago? "Send me a bill, honey, and I'll think about paying."' Penny saw his facial muscles tauten, his mouth twisting in a grim line, and she knew that he did not appreciate being reminded of what a swine he was. But she didn't care; she was fighting for her baby, her life.

'I hate to disillusion you, Raul, but all your power and all your wealth cannot pay the *bill*. You see, the price of rearing a child, a family, is love—lots and lots of love. The one commodity you cannot make or deal or buy. The one thing you do not possess and never will.'

She watched him in silence for a second. His face was like carved granite, his eyes hard, but she had the weirdest sensation that she had cut him to the quick, then quickly dismissed the thought. Nothing hurt Raul.

'You can hire your fancy lawyers, throw your money around, but you will not win. As I said before, I will allow you access, but on my terms and conditions. Take it or leave it.'

Penny thought she heard him mumble and waited, but still Raul remained silent, his dark face expressionless, so she continued, 'But that is all that is on offer, or ever likely to be...'

As a departure line, Penny thought it was rather good, and, spinning on her heel, she walked out of the room.

Lifting James up in her arms, she turned him around. 'Hello, my love, did you have a nice nap?'

'Nap, nap, nap,' James gurgled with delight.

'Not nap but nappy, I think!' Penny said ruefully, her hand on his bottom decidedly damp.

It was a simple matter to lie the little boy on the baby changer and strip off his old nappy, but not so simple to get the new one on. James loved the freedom of being half-naked. His chubby arms and legs waving around in the air, his little hand caught strands of Penny's long hair and pulled while his big brown eyes laughed happily up at her.

'Mamma, Mamma.'

'Yes, Mamma is here and always will be, I promise.' And, deftly fastening a new nappy around his dimpled bottom, she picked him up and cuddled him to her bosom. 'No strange lady—' she nuzzled his neck until he screeched with laughter '—or man is ever going to take you away from me ever again.'

'Was that for my benefit?'

Penny stopped and turned sideways; Raul was standing in the door watching them. 'No, but if the cap fits...' She trailed off.

Raul was not listening. He was gazing in rapt fascination at the child she held in her arms. She glanced down at James and, oddly, he was staring equally intently at the man. Her glance slid from one to the other; they were so alike it was uncanny.

'It's James, isn't it? I heard it on the television.' Raul's deep husky voice shook as he walked towards them.

They were the saddest words Penny had ever heard Raul utter. How appalling to have to discover your child's name from the television, and suddenly she was smitten with guilt.

'May I...? Will he let me hold him?'

His hesitant request added to the weight of her guilt. She looked up at him and saw a different Raul, stripped of all arrogance. The pleading humility in his dark gaze shocked her to her soul.

Had she done right in depriving him of all knowledge of his child? Or had she done it simply out of pride—if he did not want to marry her for herself, then she was damned if she would marry because she was pregnant? And now today she was doing the same thing again. The thought disturbed Penny more than she wanted to admit.

She forced a smile to her lips and lifted James high in the air. 'Yes, of course you can hold him,' she declared, not looking directly at Raul. 'And as for James minding you have nothing to worry about. He's such a friendly little chap he will go with anyone. Unfortunately,' she said with dry irony, recalling how easily he had toddled off with the strange woman.

Raul chuckled and, reaching out his hands, gently took James from Penny's arms. 'He may look like me but obviously he has inherited your naïve disposition.'

'I was naïve once but not any more,' Penny said quietly, not wishing to upset James but not at all happy with Raul's reminder of how easily he had fooled her years ago. But it didn't matter, because neither of the two males was listening. Raul was talking softly in Spanish to the little boy and it did not seem to matter that James did not know a word. The rapport between them was instant.

Watching father and son together brought a lump to her throat. Identical dark eyes with the exact same expression, the same curly hair. She saw James reach a chubby finger to Raul's chin and smile. Penny remembered Raul had always been a twice-a-day man when it came to shaving, sometimes three times if they had been late going to bed and he hadn't wanted to roughen her skin when making love. A vivid image of them both in the bathroom one night—Raul shaving and then sharing her shower—flashed in her mind.

She felt the colour surge in her cheeks. 'I'll go and make tea,' she said into thin air, suddenly needing to get away.

It was hard seeing her baby take so easily to Raul, she excused herself. But deep down she knew that seeing Raul again, kissing him, had awakened all the old, familiar, sensual feelings she had thought gone for ever.

He was a very dangerous man... Penny found it no easier to resist the magnetic pull of his vibrant masculinity now than she had more than two years ago, and it terrified her.

CHAPTER SEVEN

'I'M SORRY, Penny, I don't care what you say. I still don't trust him,' Amy said flatly.

Cuddling her mug of hot chocolate in one hand, with her elbow on the kitchen table, Penny propped up her head with the other hand. She was tired and she had had the same argument with Amy every night for the past four nights, ever since Raul had suggested taking Penny and James out for the day on Sunday.

'What harm can there be in going out with the man for one day?'

'I don't know. But I do know by your own admission that when Da Silva arrived out of the blue three weeks ago first he demanded marriage and then threatened a custody battle. Ask yourself, was that the action of a reasonable man? Don't forget I've seen the possessive way he holds James. He wants him, and that man is used to getting his own way—something you should know better than most . . .'

Everything Amy said was true in a way. Except now Penny did not believe that Raul had any intention of taking James away from her. Admittedly the first time he had arrived on her doorstep she had thought differently. She had been shocked rigid, and frightened. But once Raul had seen the boy he had changed from a stern-faced autocrat to doting father in minutes.

A reminiscent smile curved her lips as she saw again in her mind's eye the picture of Raul and James on the living-room floor when she had walked out of the kitchen with the tea-tray. Raul had built a castle with Lego bricks and James had been in the process of knocking it down, both of them laughing. Amy had arrived home and in her usual fiery manner had told Raul to go. To Penny's amazement Raul had gone...

But even more amazingly he had called back quite late the next evening. Amy had already left to visit her boyfriend, and Penny, alone except for James, had not known what to expect—further demands for marriage or threats of custody.

But instead Raul had been perfectly calm and correct. He'd stayed only long enough to tell her that he had spoken with his lawyer and, apart from wanting to make an allowance for James, he totally accepted her stipulation of visiting rights only, and had left with a thank-you and a promise to be in touch.

'You're not listening, are you, Penny?'

'What? Yes—yes, I am,' Penny stuttered.

'That damn man has got you mesmerised again.'

'Don't be silly, Amy. There is nothing between Raul and me any more; he treats me as he would a maiden aunt.' And it was true. On Raul's subsequent visits he had concentrated solely on James, with never a touch or glance that could be construed as the least sexual towards Penny. She was glad, she told herself, but deep down she was a bit miffed—though she would not dream of admitting it to Amy.

'I'm not so sure, girl. A leopard does not change his spots. I think he's lulling you into a false sense of security. He arrives twice a week, all very civilised and polite, plays for a few hours with the boy, then meekly leaves when you say so.'

'You worry too much.' Penny grinned at the fiery redhead's serious expression. For the first time ever in her

dealings with Raul Penny had won... It was a heady
feeling. Now Raul wanted to spend a whole day with
them and she did not see a problem.

'I know what I'm doing. By allowing Raul reasonable
access to James, strictly in my company, of course, it
might be to my advantage when the final legal arrangement is worked out. James is entitled to know his
father; I realise that now. And even you must admit Raul
is great with the boy.'

'Great with James he may be, but I still think you
should take my advice and have nothing to do with the
man until your solicitor has the arrangement signed and
sealed, strictly legit— '

'But I've already won!' Penny exclaimed in exasperation at Amy's stubbornness. 'Raul agrees with me
completely. *No* marriage, *no* messy custody battle. We
are two mature adults who had an unfortunate affair
and James was the result. Surely I can agree to spend a
day with the man for the benefit of James?' As the victor
she could afford to be generous, she thought
complacently.

'For heaven's sake, Penelope! Will you listen? You're
still in shock from the trauma of James going missing,
and Da Silva turning up like a bad penny has done
nothing to calm you down. It's understandable, but
you're not thinking straight, so please be careful.'

Amy's strident use of her full name gave Penny pause.
Was she still in shock? She didn't know. And she didn't
want to think about it. Remembering the twenty-four
hours without James hurt too much. It was enough to
know that she would never let her baby out of her sight
again if she could possibly help it.

She drained her mug and stood up. She could use an
early night, ready for the big day tomorrow.

'You're overreacting, Amy,' she said, giving her pal a reassuring hug. 'I'm off to bed, and don't worry about me; I'm fine. Tomorrow we are only going to the beach for the day. Raul is hardly likely to steal James from under my nose, now, is he?' She laughed as she left the room.

'There, my little dumpling, you're all ready.' Penny grinned and put James down on the floor. He was so sweet, dressed in a white towelling T-shirt with Mickey Mouse on the front and navy blue shorts.

'Out, Mamma.' And on chubby little legs he barrelled to the bedroom door.

Penny sighed happily and, with a last look in the mirror, picked up the holdall from the bed and followed her son down the hall. In the living room Nick was lounging on the sofa in his dressing gown. He had spent the night with Amy and looked like one very satisfied male, until James climbed on his stomach and began jumping up and down. Screams and laughter almost drowned out the persistent ring of the doorbell.

Unfastening the safety gate at the top of the stairs, and with a shouted order to Nick to hang onto James, Penny ran swiftly down and opened the door.

'Good morning, Penny.'

'Raul,' she said breathlessly. It was nothing personal, she told herself firmly. A woman would have to be dead from the neck down not to appreciate such a fine specimen of the male sex.

Gone was the businessman, the control freak, and in his place appeared a rakish, slightly disreputable character dressed in denim cut-offs, which revealed an amazing length of muscular, tanned legs, a sleeveless black T-shirt, which outlined the musculature of his broad chest, and with thick, curling hair falling over his forehead and begging for a woman's hand to brush it back.

Her eyes clung to his, and for an instant she thought that she saw a flash of savage hunger in his brilliant gaze. She took a nervous step back, then, remembering her manners, said, 'Come in.'

'You're ready on time, I see,' Raul drawled, his eyes scanning the length of her body with a very masculine interest he did not attempt to hide. 'And very nice too; slightly more voluptuous than I remember.'

'Thank you,' she said, colour surging in her cheeks. It was an old summer dress but one of her favourites— a simple scoop-necked white cotton crêpe, buttoned down the front and falling almost to her feet. Then, turning to the stairs, she added, 'I think,' not sure if she liked his 'voluptuous' comment. And for a second she wondered if he was actually trying to flirt with her.

Dismissing the thought as unlikely, she walked into the living room. Nick was rolling around the sofa with James. Penny grinned and said blithely, 'Raul, this is Nick, an almost permanent lodger.'

'Lucky man,' she heard Raul murmur, but did not see the fierce hostility in his gaze as she slipped across the room, picked up a laughing James and hugged him to her chest.

'Thank God for that!' Nick exclaimed in mock relief. 'The little terror almost permanently impaired my masculinity.'

Penny chuckled. 'I sincerely doubt that, Nick.' And, still smiling, she added for the baby's benefit, 'Come on, darling; we're off to the beach,' and spun around.

'Allow me.' Raul was in front of her, reaching for the child, and when he put his large hands around James

she flinched away because the backs of his hands seemed
to linger against her breasts in a deliberate caress.

Shocked by the rush of feeling Raul's touch evoked,
she worried her bottom lip with her teeth. The last thing
she needed was a return to the besotted girl she had once
been around him. A rather subdued Penny picked up
the holdall with all the baby paraphernalia inside and
followed Raul downstairs and out onto the pavement.

It was a beautiful, sunny early September day, and
Penny's good humour and common sense returned when
she saw Raul's sleek Jaguar parked next to Sense and
Sensibility's rather beaten-up old estate car. They really
had nothing in common except James. 'We'll have to
take my car,' she said with a grin, 'because the baby seat
is—'

'That will not be necessary. I have a baby seat in my
car.' Raul looked down at her, an unreadable expression
in his eyes. 'And everything else James might need.'

A trickle of sensation slithered down her spine. She
didn't know why but some warning instinct in her subconscious was clamouring to be heard. Penny shook her
head. She had been listening to Amy's dire warnings for
far too long. 'You certainly think of everything,' she
finally responded.

'Yes.'

She watched in astonishment as, without any help from
her, James was safely fastened into a baby carrier sus-
pended across the front passenger seat of the elegant
car. The holdall was taken from her unresisting hand,
and somehow she found herself in the back seat. A wry,
self-mocking smile tilted her wide mouth. So much for
her idea that Raul was trying to flirt with her. She felt
like a spare wheel!

Raul manoeuvred the big car out into the mainstream of traffic with easy grace, and they glided along a country lane with Raul talking softly all the time to James.

After about fifteen minutes of being ignored Penny spoke rather loudly to the back of Raul's head. 'I thought we could go to St Austell. There's quite a nice beach there.'

He cast a quick glance over his shoulder and, turning back to the road, said, 'Not to worry, Penny, I have it all planned. We are going to Fowey, and there I have hired a motor cruiser, so we can cruise along the coast and, hopefully, find a quiet beach for our picnic.'

She wanted to object, but, looking up, she met the lancing glitter of his gaze in the driving mirror and her heart leapt as her mind went blank.

Suddenly she was aware of the faint, familiar, teasing scent of his aftershave—very male, very arousing in the close confines of the car. Penny gritted her teeth. What was happening to her today? She looked at the man and got an adrenalin surge that made her thoughts go haywire. It had to stop...

She shrugged her shoulders and concentrated all her attention on the passing scenery. It sounded a perfectly reasonable plan in any case, she thought as she justified her spineless acceptance of Raul's itinerary.

Five hours later, she was glad she had accepted it. Clad in a plain black Lycra swimsuit, she lay stretched out on an air-bed on the deck of the cabin cruiser. And what a cabin cruiser! she thought drowsily, her eyes closed. It was a good forty feet long and luxuriously appointed. James was down below in one of the four cabins, having his afternoon nap, and Penny had just finished a wonderful lunch.

It had been a perfect day. Raul had found a private beach and anchored; they had spent hours playing with James in the sea and sand, only returning to the boat for a late lunch.

She smiled at her earlier misgivings. Raul certainly was not trying to flirt with her—quite the reverse; he had treated her much the same as James. No sexual innuendos, no telling glances. It was her own over-active libido that was the problem, not Raul's, she thought ruefully.

'Would you like some more wine, Penny?' a deep voice drawled in her ear, and Penny's eyes flew open.

'No, no, I think I've had enough.' She tried to pull herself up into a sitting position but didn't seem to have the strength.

'Feeling sleepy?'

A near-naked Raul kneeling over her should have intimidated her, but, looking up at him through half-closed eyes, all she could think of was how gorgeous he looked—all bronzed muscle and sinew, brief black trunks cupping his masculinity. A vivid image of another time, another place—the swimming pool at the *hacienda* filled her mind. Their naked bodies entwined. She closed her eyes against the pain of regret for the past, for what they had once shared.

She never saw the golden shards of savage triumph in his dark eyes. She never felt his strong arms close around her and carry her down below. She was asleep!

She heard the voices. It wasn't English. Spanish, maybe. She tried to open her eyes but a stabbing pain in her head put an end to the attempt; instead she groaned and rolled over. A niggling knowledge that she should be doing something hovered on the edge of her mind, but she was too tired to care and, sighing, she sank back into the arms of sleep.

The muted voices, the gentle rocking of the boat had ceased, but she was conscious of movement. Her lids felt heavy but she forced her eyes open and found herself in the very real arms of Raul. She tried to speak, but her tongue was stuck to the roof of her mouth—a mouth that was as dry as sandpaper.

There was a sinking sensation in her stomach, and for a moment she thought that she was going to be sick. Then she felt the soft mattress at her back, and she lay like a rag doll, staring up at the impassive face of the man bending over her. 'Raul.' She swallowed hard. Too much wine! Raul had carried her down to the cabin to sleep it off, she thought muzzily.

'Don't try to talk.'

'James—where...?'

'He is fine—in bed, fast asleep.'

Penny finally got her eyes to focus properly on his, and an inexplicable fear washed over her. 'Fine' he had said, but the glinting black eyes held a hard edge of cruelty that made her doubt if he was telling the truth. She looked down, and it was then she noticed that he had changed from his swimming trunks into a dark suit and white shirt. He was wearing a tie! On a boat!

She glanced quickly around the cabin. Only it wasn't the cabin. With a slowly dawning horror she recognised the room—the white walls, the crucifix on the wall above a massive antique dressing table, the huge four-poster bed. It could not be... Her aching head screamed. But it was. Raul's bedroom in the *hacienda*. She must be dreaming. She closed her eyes for a second and slowly opened them again. Nothing had changed...

Raul stood over her, a glass of water in his hand. 'Here, drink this; you will feel better,' he commanded and, sliding an arm under her shoulders, he hauled her up the bed and held the glass to her lips.

Penny was too weak to resist and drank greedily of the proffered water. When the glass was empty Raul withdrew his arm and straightened up. Penny flopped back against the pillows, her mind spinning like a windmill. She had thought that losing James for a day was the worst thing that could possibly happen to her, but waking up in Raul's bedroom in his home in Spain must run a close second.

It was a nightmare; it had to be. In a minute she would wake up, she told herself firmly, and, taking a few long, deep breaths, she dragged herself upright in the bed.

It was no nightmare. Raul stood a couple of feet away, watching her with hard eyes.

'Feeling better?' he prompted coldly.

Her head felt like lead and her heart like stone, but her uppermost emotion was an icy, fear-filled anger. But she dared not let him see that. She made herself move, sliding her legs over the side of the bed. She had to think, and think fast. She didn't know how Raul had done it. How had he got her here? Her dress bunched up around her thighs and she pulled it down over her knees, her brain spinning on oiled wheels. Wait a minute—she remembered wearing her swimsuit and lying on the air-bed on the deck of the cruiser, Raul kneeling over her, offering her more wine and asking her if she was sleepy...

'You bastard!' she exclaimed as it hit her. The swine must have drugged her and stripped her naked before slipping her briefs and dress back on.

'No. But you dared to make my son a bastard,' Raul drawled, his dark eyes flicking over her with contempt. 'And I will never forgive you for that.'

Fury raged inside her as she stared at him, her face running through the whole gamut of emotions from fear to seething hatred. She struggled to her feet and swayed slightly, but sheer rage made her move; she wanted to hit him, claw his mocking eyes out. But she stopped a foot away from him. She clenched her hands at her sides in impotent fury. James! Raul had her son. She did not dare attack him.

'Why? How?' she asked through clenched teeth.

Raul gave her a chilling smile. 'I told you I wanted my son.' He shrugged. 'I have my son.'

She stared at him with growing terror. He made it sound so simple, a fact. 'You can't possibly hope to get away with it,' she said urgently. 'The penalty for kidnapping is a long jail sentence and I will delight in giving evidence against you.'

'I think not,' Raul sneered.

'You think you are so bloody omnipotent,' Penny swore in panic. 'But James and I have friends. Already Amy will be searching for us.' Raul took a step towards her, his large hands curving around her shoulders, his fingers digging into her flesh, burning her like a brand. Her pulse beat a frightening, erratic rhythm. 'Let—' Let me go, she had been going to say, but didn't get the chance.

'No, she won't,' Raul cut her off, his black eyes narrowed venomously on her pale face, 'because, my dear Penny, you sent Amy a telegram, informing her that the trauma of losing James had finally caught up with you and you were going on holiday for two weeks.'

'Amy will never believe that,' she said, appalled at his duplicity.

Raul shrugged. 'She does not have to, but the police will.' He gave her a chilling smile laced with mockery. 'I informed the local constabulary that I was taking you on holiday to get away from the publicity et cetera. It was common knowledge in the community that I had been visiting you and James quite amicably for the past few weeks; what could be more natural?'

The full horror of her situation was finally getting through to Penny. Machiavelli had had nothing on Raul. Even to her, the victim of his diabolical plot, his explanation seemed believable. 'But what about passports, Customs? You can't just smuggle two people into a country.' She shook her head in stunned disbelief. This could not be happening to her.

Raul's mouth twisted. 'But I have,' he drawled with cynical amusement. 'You were my wife, who had overindulged in wine, and I unfortunately could not find your passport. As for James… It was quite simple; I obtained a copy of his birth certificate as soon as I knew of his existence, and discovered you had deliberately left the father's name blank.' His voice became a savage snarl. 'An oversight, Penny?' His black eyes accused her. 'But with the help of a high government official James has been registered as my son on my passport.'

'You planned this right from the first,' Penny whispered in horror, finally recognising the enormity of his deceit. Raul had let her think that she had won, that she was in control. But all the time he had been plotting to abduct the pair of them.

'Naturally.'

An icy hand gripped her heart at the one curt word. Was there no end to her stupidity? How quickly she had forgotten that during their affair Raul had always been the dominant one, in complete control. Oh, he had said that they were partners, but he'd never actually meant it. The few times she had tried to assert herself she had never really succeeded. Two years apart had taught her nothing where Raul was concerned. Amy had been right all along. He was not to be trusted...

'You're mad, Raul; stark, staring bonkers,' she said flatly, determined to stand up to him this time. If she was to have any chance of getting away with her son she could not afford to lose her temper. 'You do realise that tomorrow or the next day or even—God forbid!—two weeks from now I will walk out of here with my child?' She had to make him see reason, but the bitter hostility in his eyes was not very reassuring.

'You, maybe—James, never,' he drawled crushingly. 'My lawyer agreed that you would probably win a custody battle in England, but now you are in Spain. My country. You are an illegal immigrant with no passport. *You* might consider me mad but to everyone here I am a pillar of the community. Need I say more?'

She shuddered, his words chilling her to the bone. She had a horrible conviction that he might be right.

'You're cold, Penny,' Raul drawled silkily, his strong hands rubbing her shoulders while his dark eyes mocked her. He knew perfectly well that it was not the air temperature making her shudder. 'Why don't you have a shower and change into something fresh? This is a very nice dress, but you have been wearing it for almost two days.'

Penny dropped her head to hide the fury she knew he would see in her eyes. 'What day is it?' she managed to ask, when what she really wanted to do was murder him on the spot.

'Monday evening.' His hands slowly slipped down her arms and closed around her wrists, then he stepped back, holding her arms out wide. His mocking gaze traced slowly over her face and then lowered to linger on the creamy mounds of her breasts revealed by the low neck of the crumpled summer dress. 'The clothes you left behind are in the wardrobe. You should be able to find something that still fits you.'

Penny stiffened; to be told that she was fatter was just about the last straw. Her blue eyes shooting fire, she looked at him and caught a disturbing flash of something very like sensual anticipation in his glittering glance. She bit her lip and swallowed the angry retort. She was not strong enough to fight with Raul, not yet... Instead she looked past him and said, 'First I want to see James.'

'I've told you, he is fine. Ava and I put him to bed an hour ago.' Raul still had possession of her wrists and he moved them around her back. Linking his fingers with hers, he eased her closer. 'You are the one who needs looking after,' he purred, his breath hot on her ice-cold face.

He loomed over her, oozing a menacing animal sexuality that threatened more than words could ever do. Penny arched back, terrified of what he might do to her. 'Please, I want to see James.'

'Later,' he said with savage softness. 'I swore when you walked out on me that I would get even some day.' He jerked her hands up her back, forcing her hard against his tough body. She looked into his eyes and trembled at the implacable intent she saw there. 'And when I discovered the full extent of your betrayal I was doubly determined to make you suffer.'

With one hand he held both of hers, and with the other he roughly gripped her chin. 'I have waited a long time for this.'

'You won't get away with it,' she croaked. The hard heat of his body, his dark eyes full of hate, burning into hers, horrified her. He had fooled her completely, not just with James but by pretending that he was no longer sexually interested in her. It was in his eyes, the hard thrust of his masculine arousal against her stomach. But, worse, she had fooled herself. A pulse leapt in her throat, fire spread through her veins. She gasped for breath.

'I already have,' he grated mockingly, his mouth descending on her parted lips with a cruel passion that seemed to demand her total surrender, his tongue delving into the moist heat, forcing a response she was helpless to control.

'Oh, no,' she groaned when he allowed her to breathe, terrified by the fierce tide of pleasure flowing through her body.

'Yes, yes, yes,' Raul ground out, his hand slipping between them, down the front of her dress, to curve around the swell of her breast. A hopeless moan escaped from her parched throat and Raul stared cynically down at her flushed face. 'You're desperate for a man, Penny,' he said callously, his long fingers stroking over the already rigid tip of her breast—stroking, playing with the hard nub as he watched her with dark, mocking eyes. 'Your Nick is obviously not keeping you satisfied.'

'Nick...?' she moaned, not knowing what he was talking about.

A blinding flash of fury glittered in his eyes and roughly he grasped her breast before pushing her away from him. 'You dare to moan his name, you bitch?'

Shocked out of her emotional stupor, Penny licked her dry lips. 'I was...' But something so primitive, so sinister in Raul's eyes made her throat close, and she could not speak.

'You have the nerve to allow a man to stay overnight in the same house as my son. I could kill you for that.' He swore violently in Spanish before adding, '*Dios*! You disgust me; you're little better than a whore.'

His comment hung in the air. Penny tensed, lifting hurt, angry eyes to his, about to explain who Nick was. But she caught a flash of bitter black hatred in his eyes before he wiped all trace of expression from his hard face. She stopped. She did not owe Raul an explanation. She did not owe him anything. Instead, anger surfacing, she shot back, 'Then why, as I disgust you, did you drug me and bring me here?'

'Lucky for you, James insisted on visiting his sleeping mamma every couple of hours. Otherwise, believe me, I would have thrown you overboard in the Bay of Biscay without a second thought.' And, spinning on his heel, he walked out of the bedroom, slamming the door behind him.

CHAPTER EIGHT

PENNY looked around the room and then back to the door, not quite believing what had happened. She crossed to the bathroom and, entering, slipped off her dress and briefs.

What was that favourite saying of her local hairdresser? 'It's a treat to be alive.' How true, she thought with a wry chuckle, her irrepressible sense of humour coming to her rescue. According to Raúl, she could have been fish bait by now!

She stepped into the double shower stall, still laughing. But very quickly her laughter turned to hysteria. Tears flooded her eyes and rained down her cheeks. Her head ached, her heart ached, and as she stood under the warm shower spray, her tears mingling with the water, she had never felt so hopelessly lost in her life.

At least when James had been missing she'd had hope and the support of other people to sustain her. Now she was trapped in Raúl's house, miles from anywhere, with no friends. She had no illusions as to the loyalty of his servants, Ava and Carlos. In this part of the world the feudal system still lingered. There was no way they would help her against the master. It wasn't in their nature, and Penny had a sneaky suspicion that Ava would consider her action in withholding her son from Raúl as pretty despicable in any case.

She turned the tap on harder. As steam filled the stall she tilted her head back and closed her eyes, allowing the water to wash away her tears. Crying was not going to help her now. If only she did not feel so weak. But then being drugged would do that to one every time, she thought wretchedly.

She did not hear the shower door open, and when two strong male hands clasped her slender waist she almost jumped out of her skin. Her eyes flew open and she was looking at the broad, naked chest of a man. She did not need to see his face. She would have known the touch of those hands in her sleep, she realised bitterly.

'I thought you might need some help washing your back.' Raul's deep, mocking voice echoed in the enclosed area.

'Get out!' she cried, lifting her hands to sweep her wet hair from her face, the better to see what the hell he thought he was doing!

His head bent and his mouth fastened on her parted lips with unerring accuracy as his hands slid over her bottom and pressed her close against him.

For a moment she was stunned by the flood of emotion, the memories his kiss evoked. Her mouth welcomed him as a lover, her nipples throbbing against his hard chest, and then she realised what she was inviting and, with a sudden twist, was out of his arms, her back to him, her heart pounding erratically. 'Get out,' she spluttered, swallowing half the shower spray.

'You don't mean that, Penny.' Raul's arm closed around her slender waist, hauling her back hard against him even as his free hand snaked up to cup her breast, kneading it gently, his long fingers sliding teasingly over the hard peak in a caress that made her shudder in instant reaction.

She was immediately made aware of his hard, naked body at her back, the stirring of masculine arousal against her buttocks. 'I do,' she got out shakily. The water pounding down on her overheated body, combined with the feeling of being completely surrounded by Raul, was making her head spin.

She grasped the arm around her waist, trying to prise herself free, but as she did so, with his other hand, he rolled her aching nipple between his index finger and thumb, sending shafts of fierce, achingly familiar pleasure from her breast to her loins, while his dark head bent and his mouth nuzzled her neck, his teeth biting lightly into the tender flesh.

'You do what, Penny?' he asked, biting her ear-lobe then licking inside with his tongue. 'Ache for me, burn for me?' he whispered in an oddly gentle voice.

She sensed a subtle change in him from his earlier, raging hatred, but it made no difference; this was one fight she dared not let him win. 'No. No,' she denied desperately, her fingers digging into the flesh of the arm at her waist, but he held her manacled to his hard length in a band of steel.

'Little liar. You love it, you know you do; and turning your back on me physically or mentally won't help. You tried that once before and it almost ended in tragedy,' he cynically reminded her, all the time his teeth grazing her neck even as his long fingers glided from one aching breast to the other, plucking, playing with the rigid tips with devastating expertise. 'But never mind, my sweet, luscious Penny,' he continued in a husky whisper. 'I won't let it happen again. I'll take care of you, protect you.'

Penny bit back a moan, and trembled with each practised movement of his fingers. She tried to tell herself that she hated him, despised him. But her eyes closed and she swayed back against him, pleasure overwhelming her rational mind.

She was transported back in time to when she had lived only for Raul. His mouth on her flesh was warm, sensual and so achingly familiar. His huskily murmured erotic words against her throat should have shamed her, but instead they inflamed her senses to fever pitch.

'Nothing has changed; you still want me,' he rasped, his other hand sliding from her waist down over her belly, his fingertips parting the soft blonde curls, seeking the moist inner skin. Her hands fell to her sides and with a will of their own curved against hard, masculine thighs; her head fell back on his broad chest, and this time she could not hold back the groan.

'That's it, Penny; let go,' Raul coaxed huskily. 'I know what you want, *querida*. What you need.' He moved so that his back was to the wall, still holding her captive, his tantalising fingers caressing her breasts and the silken centre of her femininity with rhythmic, sliding strokes.

Her fingers dug into the hard flesh of his thighs as wave after wave of sensation arced through her naked body. She wanted to scream at the humiliation, while her body begged for his touch.

Raul's mouth closed on her ear, biting and nibbling, and then went to her throat; she turned her head blindly to the side to give him easy access. She was lost, burning up with a fever of the flesh that only Raul could assuage. Her breath caught in her throat. 'Please don't—' was as far as she got when his fingers slid further into her body.

'Don't do this?' he rasped against her neck as the hand at her breast slid to her waist, holding her hard against his rampantly aroused male strength. 'When you do this to me?' he growled, and she knew that she was defeated; she could no more stop him than stop the tide, and, worse, she did not want to...

His wickedly caressing fingers trailed over her tiny nub of passion with exquisite, spiralling delicacy, and shudder after shudder claimed her slender body.

'Please... stop,' she gasped, in a last futile attempt to deny her own hopeless surrender to his sensual mastery of her quivering body.

'Never,' Raul husked, and in one lithe movement he spun her around in his arms, somehow managing to turn off the water at the same time.

With dazed, passion-glazed eyes she stared up into his dark face, her whole body one seething mass of frustrated desire. He lay back against the wall and curved an arm around her waist as his other hand slid up through the tangle of her long hair and then down her spine to stroke over her buttocks and haul her into the cradle of his thighs, making her even more aware of his blatant male arousal.

'Now—say you don't want me. I dare you,' Raul goaded silkily, supremely confident of his virile masculine power. Her eyes widened on his; she saw the simmering passion in the deep black pupils, overlaid with pure male triumph, and some of the mist cleared from her bemused mind.

Sensing her partial withdrawal, Raul bent his dark head and found her lips with his, thrusting his tongue into the moist depths of her mouth. She trembled, then meekly opened to him, her tongue stroking his, wanting him as she had before. More so, with the memory of more than two long, frustrating years to fuel her desire.

Raul ended the kiss and trailed a row of tiny, nibbling bites down her throat. 'I've waited years for this. Too long...' he growled throatily. 'Touch me, Penny. Touch me as you used to.'

Blindly she reached out and ran her slender hands up over his hair-roughened chest, across the broad shoulders, down again to his hard, flat stomach. It was as if the lonely years apart had never been. With tactile delight she relished the familiar, utterly masculine form.

Her head fell back as his lowered and his mouth closed over her aching, pouting breast. He tugged on the swollen nipple and her small hand slid lower to trace his essential maleness... He was so smooth, satin over steel, so powerful, and so ready...

'That's it, Penny. Oh, yes,' he grated as his head moved from one breast to the other. His large hands curved around her buttocks and lifted her from the floor. Penny grabbed for his neck, for a second sure that she was going to fall backwards, but Raul held her firm. 'Wrap your legs around my waist. Do it, Penny,' he commanded huskily, and she did.

She clung to him while his satin strength found her, slowly, lightly. His sensuous mouth sought hers and kissed her long and hard as all the while he moved easily, softly against her, enough to tease, to stoke the fire of her passion, but not enough to quench the flame, until she wanted to scream for his possession.

'Tell me what you want, Penny. Say it. Tell me you want me,' Raul demanded raspingly over and over again, his mouth skimming from her lips to her breasts and back again, all the time his lower body moving barely an inch against her feminine core.

A streak of fire shot through her and she burned with an exquisite pleasure-pain that stopped her breath. She was hot and wet and shivering with desire. She clasped her hands around his head, holding him to her breast. Her shapely legs locked higher around his waist, trying to force her ultimate union, but Raul would not be hurried.

She could feel the straining, steely length of him against her, but he refused her the satisfaction she craved. She pressed hard, desperate kisses to his neck, his shoulder, his chest—anywhere she could reach. Her slender fingers curled in the soft dark hair of his head, pulling, making her own demand in a frenzy of need.

'I have to hear you say it, *querida*,' he grated, his great body rigid with tension, his biceps bulging as he fought to support Penny and control his own overpowering need. His head reared back, his dark eyes, black with passion, clashed with hers. 'Say it...' he demanded hoarsely. The skin pulled taut over his high cheekbones and his tanned face flushed dark red with the effort of controlling his passion.

She saw the muscle jerking spasmodically in his jaw, the sensuous line of his hard mouth; she felt his slight movement, the tip of his masculine strength teasing the centre of her desire, and she went up in flames, twisting her hips in a last desperate plea.

'I want you, Raul. I want you,' she groaned, and gasped as he arched suddenly against her, spearing her with a hot, hard, pulsating passion. 'Raul!' She cried his name as he filled her completely.

Pleasure, fever, fire. There was no word to begin to describe the feeling as Raul moved inside her with slow, deliberate strokes, and still his mouth caught her breast. His strong hand clasped her buttocks, and she cried out as his other hand slid between their two bodies and touched her there—where they were joined. Penny felt as if she was falling apart, melting all over him. Never had it been like this. Somehow he was on the floor and

she was splayed across his lap, and still he teased and
drove her wild.

She was losing her mind. His long fingers seemed to
be everywhere. She was riding a roller coaster, shuddering on the brink of oblivion, and then with a mighty
lurch he held her hard down on his all-powerful body.
She never heard herself scream; all she was aware of was
the agonising pleasure as her inner muscles convulsed
around the hard length of him and she was thrown into
another dimension, burning up, consumed by the violence of their mutual, shattering release.

Her head fell against his chest; she could hear the
heavy pounding of his heart as she fought to breathe.
His arms came around her, and for a second she believed that they were still lovers, with no secrets between
them. But slowly, as her mind began to clear, the reality
of what had happened sank into her tired brain.

They were still joined in the most intimate way. They
should have been as close as it was possible for two
people to be. But sadly, Penny realised, it was no longer
possible. In the old days they would have laughed
together to find themselves sprawled on the shower floor,
Raul would have carried her into the bedroom...

'Are you all right?' he asked flatly.

The demand broke through her passion-dazed mind.
She lifted her head; her blue eyes met Raul's guarded
glance—not a glint of humour between them.

She fought to contain her erratic breathing, to be as
cool as Raul. 'If you call being assaulted all right, then,
yes, I am fine,' she finally answered sarcastically, and
tried to move.

In one lithe movement Raul stood up, taking her with
him and planting her firmly on her own two feet in front
of him. The fact that they were both naked did not seem

to faze him one bit, but suddenly Penny was overcome with embarrassment. She tried to step out of the cubicle, but Raul's hand on her arm stopped her.

'There was no assault, Penny. So don't bother trying to lay the guilt trip on me, because it will not wash. You wanted me. You begged me, and don't you forget it.'

He was angry; she could see it in the dark glitter in his gold-flecked eyes, in the tension in his huge body. 'And who made me beg?' she shot back, slowly regaining some control of her shocked senses. Pulling her arm free with a toss of her proud if somewhat bedraggled head, she forced her trembling legs to move and slipped out of the shower. He was right, but there was no way she was going to admit it.

She grabbed a large bath towel off the rail and wrapped it around her shivering body; suddenly she was cold, both inside and out. She needed to get away, get some space to think. But before she could leave the bathroom Raul was once again at her side.

She blinked and glanced warily at him through lowered lashes. At least he'd had the decency to wrap a towel around his hips; though, in all honesty, she had to admit that he looked great in anything or nothing! The breadth of his bronzed shoulders, the hair on his chest, exaggerating the perfect muscle structure, his narrow waist and slim hips were an enticement to any red-blooded female. God! She was doing it again—getting carried away on the physical. Would she never learn?

'Have I grown a pair of horns and a tail?' Raul drawled sardonically, fully aware of her veiled scrutiny.

'You were always a devil, if that's what you mean,' Penny blurted out recklessly, hating his mockery almost as much as she hated him. 'You had no right to invade my privacy in the shower and you know it.'

'It wasn't only your privacy I invaded, and very nice it was too,' he chuckled.

The swine was laughing at her; he actually thought that her complete surrender to his sexual persuasion was amusing. 'I wouldn't know; being under the influence of drugs probably has that effect on one,' she said scathingly, and, pushing past him, fled to the bedroom.

But Raul was only a step behind her. 'Drugs had nothing to do with it,' he snarled, catching her around the waist and swinging her around to face him. 'Why can't you be honest and admit that whatever has happened between us in the past, however much you hate me, I only have to touch you and you want me almost as much as I want you. Or is honesty from a woman too much to hope for?' he demanded angrily.

'Oh, I see, and it's honest to kidnap someone, steal their child and then seduce them?'

Raul ran a hand through his hair, an expression of disgust twisting his rugged features. 'For God's sake, Penny! We have just made love; it had to happen; the chemistry—call it what you will—is there between us all the time. You know it. I simply decided we should get it over with and then get down to the real business of arranging our son's future.'

'*My* son. And if you don't mind I would like to get dressed and go and see him.'

'It will not work, Penny; you can try as hard as you like, but James is our son and in my home—where he is going to stay.'

Bristling with anger, Penny stared up into his hard face. 'Two weeks holiday, you said, and then we are out of here.'

'I lied; you are not leaving, and, God willing, in nine months' time James might have a brother or sister.'

Penny's mouth fell open with shock.

'You'll catch flies like that,' Raul drawled mockingly, his dark eyes lit with amusement.

'You swine, you did that deliberately.'

'Well, last time it only took the one night in Dubai; I have no reason to suppose this time will be any different.'

Poleaxed did not begin to describe Penny's feelings. It had never once occurred to her that she might get pregnant again, and she squashed the flicker of pleasure the thought of another child gave her. She would not give Raul the satisfaction.

'A shakedown in the shower is hardly likely to end up in pregnancy,' she said flippantly.

'A shakedown...' Raul shook his dark head in disbelief. '*Dios*! You have changed. The young girl I once knew would never have spoken that way.'

'The naïve, besotted fool you once knew no longer exists,' Penny snapped back, glad to have jolted him for a change.

'Did I read you all wrong in the past, Penny? Were you really besotted?' His dark eyes caught and held hers, and just for a second she was tempted to tell him the truth.

But she saw the expectant gleam in his eye, and she was damned if he was going to win again. Instead she straightened her shoulders and strolled across the room, opening drawers willy-nilly until miraculously she found some underwear.

'No answer, Penny? It is unlike you to be stuck for words.' His mocking voice infuriated her and, struggling into briefs and a bra, she let the towel fall to the floor before turning to face him.

He was standing leaning against the dressing table, still wearing only a towel and looking impossibly smug.

'What's to say? The past is past. Now, where did you say my clothes were?'

'At my instruction, Ava transferred all the clothes you left in the guest room and the dressing room to the antique wardrobe over there.' She saw him flick a long hand in the direction of the huge mahogany cupboard.

Penny did not like the sound of that. Where exactly was she supposed to sleep? She bit her lip but made no comment; instead, moving to the wardrobe, she flung back the door and eyed the row of dresses, trousers and sweaters she had left behind two years ago.

Grabbing the first garment—a pale blue shift dress—she pulled it quickly over her head, doing her best to ignore Raul's brooding presence. Smoothing the sleek blue fabric over her slender hips, she glanced across at his lounging figure. But he wasn't finished with her yet.

'But the past is not past for you and me, Penny.' Raul gave her a feral grin. 'We have a very lively son, and maybe more in the future.'

She did not need reminding again of how careless they had been. 'For me the past is over, and, as for the present, if I get pregnant then you and Nick will have to have a blood test.' Swallow that one, buster, she thought mutinously. So far Raul had had everything his own way. It was time he had something to sweat over for a change. But to her amazement he burst out laughing.

'I'm glad you find it funny,' she said flatly. 'But the joke might be on you in nine months' time.'

'Nice try, Penny. An hour ago I might have believed you. But young James is a very intelligent little boy.'

'Even you wouldn't stoop so low as to question a young boy little more than a baby.'

Straightening to his full height, Raul stalked across the room and stopped a pace away from her. 'I did not have to. I looked in on him before joining you in the shower. He was quite talkative. Apparently he sleeps with you, and Uncle Nick sleeps with Amy.'

She felt a fool; the colour surged in her face and she could not look at Raul. Instead she deliberately changed the subject.

'I need a drink or something—the after-effect of whatever poison you gave me, no doubt. I feel sick to the stomach.' And she did, but only she knew that it was with shame—shame that she had given in to Raul's lovemaking, shame because her own innate honesty forced her to admit that she had enjoyed it.

His hand came out and gripped her wrist as she would have walked past him. A current of feeling ran through them, linking them in an electric tension. 'Not so fast, Penny.'

'Let go of me,' she said, raising her eyes to his.

Raul smiled unpleasantly. 'No.'

For a long moment her eyes skimmed the hard features of the man she had once loved, the man whose child she had borne, and she wondered how she could have allowed herself to be so easily deceived a second time. 'Let me go.'

Something ugly moved in the golden-flecked eyes, but no hint of emotion disturbed the harsh angles of his handsome face. His fingers tightened painfully on hers. 'Never,' he said softly, silkily. 'And let me make one thing quite clear—I checked with a doctor and the two pills I gave you were quite harmless, simple sleeping pills. Yours in fact.'

'Mine?' she exclaimed in astonishment.

'Yes; the ones your doctor left for you when James was stolen. I took them from your bathroom cabinet.'

The audacity and cunning of the man left Penny speechless. It was almost funny! But one glance at Raul's set face told her that now was not the time to laugh, as he continued, his voice hard and heavy with derision, 'So don't try and blame a supposed drug for what happened in the shower. You wanted me. However much you say you hate me, however you try and defy me, both you and I know the chemistry between us is still as powerful as the night we met.'

Her lashes fluttered down; she could not hold his gaze without giving away the truth. He was right.

'Because of that, and because of James, I am prepared to give you a choice. You can live here with me, take up where we left off more than two years ago, or go back to England on your own. But a platonic relationship between you and me is not an option.'

Penny looked up and saw the merciless glitter in his dark eyes. 'That is no choice at all,' she said in a horrified whisper.

'It is the only choice you are going to get,' he said, with a chilling lack of emotion that made her blood run cold.

She stared up at him, the full enormity of what he had suggested slowly sinking into her emotionally battered brain. 'But...'

His dark head swooped and his mouth bruised her love-swollen lips. After a moment he lifted his head and she saw in his cold, implacable smile something sinister. She shivered, yet it was Raul who was almost naked.

'Think about it—' he dropped her hand '—while I dress for dinner.'

'But—'

'No more buts, Penny. You're beginning to sound like a parrot.' And, easily reaching past her, he pulled open a drawer.

'B—' She almost said it again, but the mocking smile he shot her as he quite casually dropped the towel from his waist and pulled on a pair of boxer shorts stopped her. 'Where is James?' she asked, avoiding looking at Raul. 'I need to see him.'

'Your old bedroom, but don't be long; dinner is in half an hour.'

Penny dashed to the cot and stared down at her sleeping son. He looked so peaceful, his little hand curled around a floppy-eared teddy bear. She bent down and pressed a swift kiss on the top of his dark curls. He murmured slightly but did not wake up. She stared at him, a host of turbulent thoughts and emotions swimming in her head.

James was such a happy, contented little chap; a small, sad smile curved her generous mouth. The little boy had no knowledge of the trauma surrounding him, and she knew that she had to keep it that way. However much she might resent and despise Raul, rage at fate that had played such a cruel trick on her, as a mother all her instincts told her that, whatever the cost to herself, James must be shielded from the quarrel between his parents.

Lifting her head, she looked around her old room; her eyes widened in amazement as she took in the surroundings. What had once been an elegant guest room was now a nursery. The huge, old-fashioned cot claimed pride of place in the centre of the room. A large rocking-horse stood under one window, and under the other stacks of toys. The wall had been painted cream and stencilled with dozens of Walt Disney characters. Suddenly the enormity of what had happened hit her...

For hours, days, weeks, even, she had been living in a kind of dream or nightmare. From the moment she'd lost her son for a day until now she had not been thinking clearly.

This room... a nursery... The boat trip... Raul had planned every move down to the finest detail. He must have started from the first moment he'd realised that James was his son. Whereas Penny had been so euphoric at getting James back that she had taken Raul at face value, had quite blindly believed him when he'd said that he would not fight for her child, had believed he had no interest in her whatsoever.

What a joke! While Penny had been congratulating herself on behaving as a mature adult, doing the right thing by her son, Raul had been plotting his every move.

Just how well he had succeeded was brought home to Penny ten minutes later when she reached the bottom of the grand staircase to be swept into the motherly arms of Ava.

In rapid Spanish Ava, with tears in her eyes, said, 'You poor, dear girl. When the master told me a wicked, wicked woman had stolen your child I could not believe it. He showed me the newspaper and I wept. But thank God the master found you and you got the baby back.'

'Ava—' Penny tried to break in but didn't get the chance.

'You are not to worry ever again. Carlos and I will guard the baby with our life and the master has hired security men for the road. You will both be perfectly safe here.'

Touched by the older woman's concern, but with a sinking feeling in the pit of her stomach, Penny responded in Spanish. 'It's good to see you again.' And, kissing Ava's weathered cheek, she meant it. But she realised with a kind of fatalistic acceptance that Raul had covered all the bases. There was no chance of Penny persuading the older woman to help her get away.

She lifted her head and Raul was standing leaning against the dining-room door, waiting for her. He was immaculately dressed in a white silk shirt and dark lounge suit, his hair brushed firmly back from his broad brow, his face cool and aloof.

'If you two ladies have quite finished your tearful reunion, I am a very hungry man.'

His dark eyes clashed with Penny's, and for a fraction of a second the coolness faded, replaced by a naked hunger of another kind. She felt her stomach curl in answering need. Then it was gone, his formidable control once more in place, and, following Raul into the dining room, she put her own reaction down to lack of food.

'Would you like a drink?' Raul asked, stopping at the long oak sideboard where a decanter and array of bottles were on display with a dozen crystal glasses.

Ignoring his question, Penny said tightly, 'Clever. Very clever, Raul. But really, a guard on the road... isn't that overdoing it a bit?'

He glanced over his shoulder to where she stood by the dining-room table, bristling with anger and resentment. 'Nothing is too good for my son; I have no intention of allowing anyone, including you, to take him away from me. Understood?'

She recognised the cold menace in his tone and knew that now was not the time to argue with him. But she did raise her head in a valiant attempt at dignity. 'In that case give me a sherry. I need one. I do not appreciate being threatened by a... a... pirate...' she blustered.

'A pirate?' Raul spun to face her, one dark brow arched sardonically. 'Really, Penny!' He almost smiled. 'A Freudian slip? A subtle invite to rape and pillage, perhaps? You are getting desperate.' And, chuckling at her gasp of outrage, he turned his attention to the drinks tray and poured sherry from the decanter, filling two glasses.

Desperate was not the half of it, Penny thought, watching him warily as he approached and held a glass out to her.

'Drink this; it might cool that vivid imagination of yours and steady your nerves.'

'I don't have unsteady nerves,' she shot back, but took the glass and sipped the fortified wine. It gave her the courage to demand, 'I want to ring Amy; she will be worried.'

Raul drained the liquid from the glass in his hand and, setting it on the table, stared down at her in a cold, assessing way for a long moment, the tension in the air growing by the second.

'All right.'

Shock kept her motionless, her brow furrowed in a puzzled frown. Raul had agreed. She had not expected it, and as she watched he walked across the room to where the phone rested on an occasional table and quickly dialled a number, and spoke. 'Raul here.'

'Wait a minute.' Galvanised into action, she dashed after him. 'Hey, wait a minute, I said.' She grabbed his sleeve; he glanced down at her hand, a wicked glint in his dark eyes.

'Hello, Amy. How are you managing on your own? Penny was worried about you. Yes . . . yes. Here she is.' But before handing Penny the receiver he bent and whispered, 'I'll be listening, and upsetting your friend will not do either of you any good.'

Penny gripped the receiver, tears hazing her eyes at the sound of Amy's voice.

'What the hell is going on, Penny? I couldn't believe the telegram. I went to the police and they said it was all above board; Raul left them his phone number if they needed to get in touch.'

This was her big chance, Penny realised. All she had to do was tell Amy the truth—she had been abducted by the father of her child. Amy would move heaven and earth to help her. Penny would probably make the news. Yet again! A bitter battle over James would ensue. She imagined the scenario, the headlines in the newspaper: *Son Abducted One Month. Mother and Son the Following Month.* She would be a laughing stock at best, and, at worst, viewed as a totally incompetent mother.

She stood with the receiver jammed to her ear. She opened her mouth but her throat closed up. She lifted pained eyes to Raul's face. There was no softening in his hawk-like regard, and she knew in that second that she could not do it. She was beaten...

'Penny? Penny, are you still there?'

She swallowed hard. 'Yes, yes, I'm still here, Amy. I'm sorry if you were worried. But I'm fine; James is fine.' Once she had told the first lie it got easier. Forcing a lightness to her tone that she did not feel, Penny continued, 'I decided at the last minute James and I needed a holiday after the abduction and everything...and R-Raul—' she stumbled over his name '—kindly offered us accommodation at his *hacienda*—'

'Kind? Raul? Are you sure?' Amy cut in suspiciously.

'Perfectly. I thought we would stay a couple of weeks. That is, if you can manage on your own.'

A dry chuckle echoed down the wire. 'You're kidding, of course! Since the new health centre opened Sense and Sensibility barely needs one pharmacist, let alone two.'

With relief Penny let Amy ramble on about the business or lack of it, and when she finally put the telephone down Penny knew that her friend was convinced that she was all right.

'Very sensible,' Raul said quietly.

Any remark Penny felt like making was halted as the housekeeper bustled into the room carrying a soup tureen.

CHAPTER NINE

DINNER had been a tense affair. Neither one of them had done justice to Ava's supposedly celebratory meal. Penny had been too busy arguing for her freedom in increasing desperation while Raul, with cold inflexibility, had refused to be moved from his original statement. She could go or stay, but James stayed...

Penny had felt her nerves winding up like a corkscrew every time she glanced across the table and met Raul's dark, implacable gaze. She was exhausted. And all she wanted to do was bury her head in the sand like an ostrich and pretend it was all a bad dream.

She had refused Raul's suggestion to take coffee in the salon, preferring the hard-backed dining chair and the width of the table between them, but as she drained her cup and replaced it on the table she could stand the tension, the stalemate no longer.

'Where exactly am I supposed to sleep?' she ground out between tightly clenched teeth as her blue eyes clashed with Raul's yet again. 'There is no bed in James's room.'

'With me, of course.'

He smiled, and she could see that he was deadly serious. Her stomach clenched in fear—and another emotion she dared not recognise. She knew just how persistent Raul could be. An attractive, virile male with wealth and power plus a single-minded, ruthless determination to get his own way was a combination almost impossible to beat, and, being brutally honest, she was no longer sure that she wanted to beat Raul... 'No,' she finally responded shakily, but she had delayed too long.

Raul had moved and was beside her, one hand on the back of her chair and the other on the table, hovering over her like some great black avenging angel. 'The nursery is for James...' he said with chilling softness. 'Alone...' And, straightening to his full height, he carelessly flicked a finger under her chin, adding, 'End of subject.'

He dismissed her as he would a child, just as he had done years ago, Penny thought, her anger rising again. 'Not so fast,' she cried, and, leaping to her feet, she caught the sleeve of his jacket as he made to leave. His black head turned and she stared up at him, tears of anger and frustration stinging her eyes, but she refused to let them fall. 'James needs me; he's still a baby,' she protested violently.

'He may need you, but he is too old to share a bedroom with his mother,' Raul declared, his eyes narrowing to skim assessingly over her slender body, the blue of the simple shift she wore reflecting in her wide, defiant eyes. 'I, on the other hand, rather like the idea.'

Penny shivered, alarm and, more shaming, an electric awareness running through her as she stared at him in silence for a second. Her heart leapt as Raul moved closer, his hand threading under her hair to clasp the back of her neck. 'You...you can't make me,' she said, fear making her stammer.

'I could, but I hope I won't need to, Penny,' he said and smiled—a cruel twist of his firm lips. 'Because you are going to sleep in my bed even if I have to carry you there myself. This is not negotiable.' And he lowered his head. Then his mouth stole her breath away.

Expecting a savage assault, she was overwhelmed by the sweet tenderness of his kiss. He held her with one hand at her nape and sipped at her lips like a man drinking the nectar of the gods. His very tenderness defeated her, her fingers curling involuntarily into the soft fabric of his sleeve.

He raised his head to look at her flushed, bewildered face and murmured, 'On the other hand...' Lifting a finger, he outlined the swollen bow of her top lip. 'This is negotiable, Penny,' he murmured with a sensual smile. 'But I give you my word I will not touch you unless you want me to. The bed is more than big enough for both of us.'

'I don't trust you,' she said, still shaken by his kiss but not taking her eyes off him.

'You can put a pillow down the middle if you want to.'

'A pillow?' she scorned. After his behaviour in the shower, she knew damn well that a pillow would not stop Raul. 'This aftern—'

'This afternoon was...' Raul grinned. 'What was it you said?' One dark brow arched teasingly. 'Ah, yes, a shakedown.'

She flushed scarlet and looked away, angry and confused. For a second she was reminded of the Raul she had first met, who had delighted in teasing her.

'Personally I think a shake*out* would be a more accurate description. It was necessary to get our anger and frustration with each other out in the open, to enable us to concentrate all our energies on making a good life for our son, without the added distraction of wondering if sex between us was still as red-hot as ever.'

Penny's cheeks burned even brighter; her hand fell from his sleeve and she glared up at him in helpless frustration. Why was the man always so damned right? It wasn't fair. 'So you say, but then you seduced me,' she hissed.

'Granted.' He had the gall to grin. 'But when you got going there was no stopping you.'

The simple truth of his statement was undeniable. She sighed and closed her eyes for a second, blocking out the brilliant intensity of Raul's mocking gaze.

'Come on, Penny.' His arm settled around her shoulders and she stiffened instinctively. But his strong hand squeezed her shoulder, not hard, but in an oddly comforting gesture as he urged her towards the door and out into the hall. He stopped at the foot of the staircase, surprising Penny by setting her free.

He glanced down into her wary blue eyes, and, curving a long finger under her chin, lifted it. 'You have nothing to worry about,' he said, holding her gaze with the first gentle look he had given her since she had returned to Spain. 'You can go to bed in the sure knowledge that I will not lay a finger on you without your consent.'

As Penny saw it, she did not have a lot of choice. She could believe him or fight, and, as she fought down a wide yawn, belief won...

How long she had spent watching her sleeping son Penny had no idea, but suddenly it seemed a matter of the utmost urgency to be in bed and asleep before Raul came upstairs.

She dashed through the preparation for bed with the speed of light, then grimaced in exasperation at her reflection in the dressing-table mirror. The only nightdress she could find was one from years back, when it had seemed important to look good for Raul. Now she thought the garment was indecent. Tiny straps over her slender shoulders supported a sliver of white silk cut on the bias to cling to every curve; the fact that her bust was a little fuller was not helped by the deep inset of the finest white lace almost to her navel.

Still, she thought, climbing into the huge bed, with a bit of luck Raul would never see it. If she got to sleep before him, and up before he was awake... God help her! Who was she trying to fool? Herself?

There was no way she was ever going to sleep. Her life had been turned upside down. She was in a foreign country, with her son in the room next door and not an idea in her head. She sighed. Her head sinking into the soft pillow, she curled her hands around the edge of the mattress, determined to take up as little space as possible. There must be something she could do... but what?

She yawned widely. The only thing she was absolutely sure of was that she would never, ever leave her son... His abduction had taught her that much. She would have given anything—her life, her soul to the devil—to get him back. Pride, money, career meant nothing in comparison to her child. She had finally realised that the reality of life was the family—nothing else mattered.

Penny stirred uneasily, her hands losing their grip on the mattress, a traitorous thought invading her tired mind. If she truly believed that, why do anything? James was safe and loved; she was safe and, if not loved, at least desired. Many a marriage was made on less. Her long lashes brushed her cheeks. The trouble was, she thought hazily, that Raul had not suggested marriage. Her eyes closed and she was asleep.

She didn't see Raul enter the bedroom and stand by the bed staring down at her sleeping form; she didn't feel the brush of his hand on her brow, pushing back her tumble of hair, but she stirred slightly at the soft kiss on her cheek, and turned over in the wide bed.

She was freezing in the blinding ice of stark white walls, the silence so total that every beat of her heart echoed in her brain. Penny moaned in her sleep, her head tossing from side to side. 'No, no,' she cried, but no sound escaped. She watched in ever mounting horror and fear as the ghostly outline of a man came towards her, the white coat moving, blending with the walls closing in on her, about to crush the life from her.

Somehow, on some level, she knew that she was in a nightmare—the same nightmare she had suffered on a regular basis since James had been kidnapped. But this time it was worse. Through a hazy mist she saw the man stop in front of her, his features changing, first fair and then inexplicably dark and suddenly fair again; she wept at the pity in his eyes. She saw his mouth open and she could not bear it, knowing what he was going to say. She screamed, 'Not James, no. No. No-o-o.'

Great, shuddering tears shook her slender body. 'Please, please . . .' she whimpered, trying to force her eyes open. Then from a long way off she heard the voice.

'Hush. Hush, *querida*; don't cry. James is safe.' She registered the warmth around her, the soft, compassionate voice saying, 'You're both safe. Nothing will ever harm you again.'

Penny sought the source of the warmth, pressing into the hard male flesh, her arm sliding over a taut, masculine waist, clinging for all she was worth. She had been so frightened, but a large, familiar hand softly stroked her brow, another tenderly rubbed her back; she was cocooned in a solid, comforting circle of heat.

Her head lay on a broad chest; she shivered on a sob and sighed, her lashes flickering in a brief attempt to open her eyes, then closing again. She heard the steady, firm beat beneath her ear—a reassuring and convincingly safe sound—and, snuggling ever closer, she drifted back to sleep.

This time there was no fear, no nightmare, just the gentle caress of warm lips on her cheek. Her throat arched, her head falling back on a soft pillow. She felt the warmth of sensuous lips across her own, the whispered words a caress against her mouth.

'Trust me; you and James are safe, now and always.' It was what she wanted to believe, so she believed. A soft, relieved sigh parted her lips as the husky voice continued, 'You're so beautiful, so perfect. The mother of my child.'

Penny shivered as the firm lips trailed down her throat, planting kisses every inch; she was no longer afraid but safe and secure in the arms of her lover. She put her hands against his chest, her palms flat, her fingers tangling in curling body hair. It was a dream, but such a perfect dream that she never wanted to wake up.

Her dream lover's hand slid over her shoulders, removing the fine straps of her gown, pushing it down around her feet with ease, his strong hands caressing her legs, her inner thigh, teasing back up her naked body, finding a creamy breast, his long fingers stroking the rosy tip into a small hard nub of desire.

She groaned. Her lashes fluttering, her own fingers returned the favour, finding a hard male nipple, plucking. And she heard an answering groan. A secret, sensual smile twitched her lips and she moved restlessly on the bed, heat flooding through to her groin, her legs parting involuntarily. One collided with a hard, masculine thigh and she moved her foot, stroking like a cat against the long, sinewed leg of her dream lover, and finally settled with her leg wrapped over his thigh.

'Do you know what you're doing to me?' a rasping voice murmured against her curved lips before slanting over her mouth, hungrily seeking the dark, moist interior with a deliciously dancing tongue.

'Hmm.' Penny moaned her agreement; after the horror of the nightmare this was a dream she could live with for ever.

But it wasn't a dream. Her eyes flew open. Raul was leaning half over her; his eyes, burning with a golden flame, stared into hers. 'You're sure?' he husked, his hand sliding down over her breast, tracing the indentation of her waist, curving around her buttock, and then she realised that her leg was still wrapped around his, and the hard evidence of his desire moved titillatingly against her feminine centre.

'Raul.' She was confused. 'Raul, I think—'

'Don't think, just feel, *querida*,' he said, and claimed her mouth with his own once again, kissing her hungrily. 'I have dreamt of having you in my bed again for so long, so many sleepless nights.' He kissed her throat, her breasts, his tongue flicking the taut, pouting nipples— first one and then the other— biting gently. The abrasive feel of his jaw against her flesh and the teasing tongue-strokes were her downfall.

Penny moaned softly, her hands trembling as one slid up his broad back, the other down over his hard male thigh; she heard his harsh indrawn breath as she urged him closer, signalling her surrender.

'*Dios*, you are perfection.' And with a low groan he settled his long body between her parted thighs and reared up on his elbows, his black eyes glittering with a golden flame. 'I could never tire of looking at you in a thousand years.' He cupped her breasts, and then he kissed each one in turn; he fell against her, his hands curving around her buttocks, lifting her bodily to accept his hard length into her eager body.

Penny gasped, not with pain but with the exquisite pleasure of having him sheathed inside her. Her dazed blue eyes, wide with wonder, looked up into the black molten depths of Raul's.

He stopped, perfectly still inside her. 'You were always mine, Penny,' he said with a ferocious growl. 'Always.' And then he began to move his hips in a slow, pulsing rhythm.

Penny clung to him, her fingers kneading, digging into his broad shoulders, scratching down his back, her body naturally joining his rhythm, and she realised that Raul was right. She was his—always had been and probably always would be. Then her mind closed down and she flew with him as he increased the pace with a driving urgency that spun them both into the explosive ecstasy of mutual fulfilment.

Hours or maybe minutes later—Penny had no idea how long they lay, their sweat-licked bodies entwined in a sated daze, their ragged breathing the only sound in the room—slowly, with dawning horror, she realised what she had done. Did she have some deep subconscious wish to get pregnant again? she thought bleakly. Or was she just a careless young woman with overactive hormones. She cringed in disgust. Raul felt her shiver and, rolling onto his back, pulled up the coverlet with one hand and slid his other arm around her shoulders, curving her into his side.

'Don't worry, Penny; we'll get married in a few days,' he drawled, in a voice deep with exhaustion and a smug satisfaction that infuriated her.

She jerked upright in the bed, digging her elbow in his chest in the process. How did he read her mind like that? she marvelled, at the same time as she resented him for being so arrogantly sure of himself. 'No way,' she snapped, staring down at him, her blue eyes flashing with fury.

With the first light of dawn infiltrating the room Raul lay on his back, gazing assessingly up at her. 'I want you and my son,' he said bluntly. 'And, considering what we have just done, marriage is the only option.'

'Just like that.' Penny waved her hand wildly in the air. 'You honestly think I will marry you simply because you're a great lover and...'

Raul chuckled and, wrapping his arms around her, pulled her down on top of him, pinning her to his broad chest. 'Thanks for the compliment, honey,' he murmured huskily, cupping the back of her head and kissing her flushed cheek.

Penny wriggled a few times but gave up when she realised that it was having an arousing effect on Raul and he was simply laughing at her. Anyway, she was too exhausted to argue and wasn't really sure she wanted to. He had called her 'honey', just like in the old times, and somehow it seemed to ease her lingering resentment.

'Go to sleep. We'll talk in the morning.' Raul stroked her back in a reassuring, non-sexual way, and she did.

But when she woke it was to the sound of childish laughter outside her window and the realisation that she was alone in the wide bed. She jumped out, pulled the coverlet around her naked body and crossed to the window.

The huge courtyard sparkled in the bright September sunlight; her gaze roamed around the familiar enclave— the patio area, the gnarled olive trees, the more formal garden with geraniums, roses, a multitude of flowers lovingly tended by Carlos, and, set in one corner, cleverly screened at ground view by a trellis with climbing hydrangeas, hibiscus and bougainvillea, the swimming pool.

From her elevated position she could see the shallow end of the pool, and her heart squeezed with emotion.

James, naked except for rubber armbands, was clinging to the broad shoulders of Raul and laughing his head off as Raul kept dunking him in the clear blue water up to his armpits and swinging him high in the air.

The sun gleamed golden on Raul's dark head and glistened on his broad back; she breathed deeply, struck by the pleasure the picture gave her. In a subdued frame of mind she slowly washed and pulled on a pair of old white shorts that she had found and a cropped blue T-shirt.

She brushed her hair, flicking it back over her shoulder, and turned back to the window. Raul and James were sitting side by side on the edge of the pool, their two dark heads close together. She sighed, and turning, sat down on the edge of the bed to slip on her sandals. She had no idea of the time but guessed that it was late. Possibly too late for her, in more ways than one...

There was no denying that James loved his father, and Raul certainly adored James. Did she have the right to keep them apart, to take James back to Cornwall and her small apartment with no garden? The *hacienda* was a marvellous place for a little boy to grow up, even she could see that.

Then there was the added worry of the consequences of unprotected sex... No, she refused to think about last night; she was exhausted and depressed, and Raul had caught her at a weak moment. But she could not quite block out the memory of Raul's passionate and, yes, tender lovemaking, or her tempestuous response. A devilish question leapt into her worried mind. Did she honestly want to go back to being a working, celibate, single mother? Never again to feel the exquisite joy of Raul's caress...

She got to her feet and finally ventured downstairs; the antique clock in the hall said twelve noon and she turned scarlet. God! she'd been in bed half the day... It was deeply embarrassing to have to meet Ava's happy, knowing smile when she walked into the kitchen.

'*Buenos días, señora.*' Ava spoke in rapid Spanish. 'The master told me not to wake you. You needed your sleep. James has been washed and fed and is perfectly happy with his papa in the pool.

'Now, what will you have to eat—an omelette or pastries? I have your favourites; the master told me to order them specially for your arrival. Or perhaps you would prefer to wait for lunch? I have made fresh coffee. Sit down and drink, and we can discuss the wedding.'

All the time she spoke Ava darted around the kitchen, placing a cup and saucer on the scrubbed table and filling it with strong, aromatic coffee. 'There is so much to arrange and so little time.'

Penny smiled; she couldn't help it, even though she was furious with Raul. Ava was brimming over with happiness and excitement. She had promoted Penny from *señorita* to *señora* overnight. She obviously thought that all her dreams had come true and that the *hacienda* once again was a happy family home; to Penny's chagrin she had not the heart to disappoint the old lady.

Not yet, anyway, she qualified in her head while answering Ava in her own language. 'Just coffee, please, Ava, and can we leave the discussion until later? I want to join James in the pool.'

Her answer seemed to please Ava even more, as with a wide grin Ava said, 'Of course. It is wonderful you miss your men so quickly.'

Never mind missing, she wanted to murder one particular male. Raul! she thought venomously as she strode across to the swimming pool. How dared he tell Ava they were getting married? Dear heaven, what if he had told James? No. She shook her head, dismissing the worry as she walked around the trellis.

'*Bonns Doss, Bonns Doss*....Mamma.' James's excited cry had her eyes flying to her child to the exclusion of everything else.

Penny held out her arms and watched as James dashed up to her. He looked so cute stark naked and slightly sunburned. 'Hello, darling.' She swept him up in her arms and planted a swift kiss on his grinning face.

'No, Mamma. *Bonns Doss, Bonns Doss*.' He wriggled to be put down, and, bending, Penny set him back on his feet, a puzzled frown on her face.

'*Bonns Doss*?' she repeated quizzically. Usually James was an excellent speaker.

'*Buenos Días*, Penny.'

At the sound of Raul's voice she slowly straightened up. He was standing very close and she was treated to a view of long, sinewy legs planted slightly apart, brief black swimming trunks that did nothing to hide his masculine attributes, and acres of muscular chest. Her face was flushed by the time she raised her eyes to his.

'I have been teaching James Spanish. *Bonns Doss*...is his version of *buenos días*.' And Raul grinned. 'Not bad for a first attempt, hmm?'

She wanted to be angry, but instead she found her lips twitching in the beginning of a smile. 'I should have guessed. Trust you to waste no time.'

'I've wasted too much time already,' Raul said, and she thought she saw a flicker of pain in his dark eyes before his usual control blanked his rugged features.

'You certainly have not with Ava,' Penny tossed back, suddenly reminded of her reason for facing Raul. 'How dare you tell her to arrange a wedding?'

'Not in front of the child. Wait here,' he said curtly, and, picking James up, strolled off towards the house.

She had never in her life met a man with such a penchant for rapping out orders, Penny thought mutinously. She had half a mind to follow him, but she hesitated. She needed to talk to him, and if they were out in the open there was less chance of her ending up in his arms.

She flopped down on a convenient lounger, and, drawing up her legs, hugged them. Resting her chin on her knees, she stared moodily out over the swimming pool.

After James had been abducted she had sworn never to let him out of her sight. It was ironic that she had hardly spent any time with him in the past two days. But worse, she realised sadly, James was happy, and as well if not better looked after by Raul and his staff and the protection his money could offer. Penny could not hope to compete.

Compete. The word lingered uneasily in her mind. Did she want to compete with Raul for her son's love? Parenting should mean that the mother and father were equally concerned and caring for the child, and yet, to her shame, she had positively gloated over the past few weeks, because she'd thought she had *won* over Raul. There was no winner when a child was deprived of a parent.

Years ago she had loved Raul and asked him to marry her, and because he had not leapt at the chance she hadn't told him that she was pregnant. It had been pain and pride that had prevented her telling him the truth. She had been young and idealistic about love; now she realised that there were many shades of love. She loved James desperately, she loved Amy deeply, and she loved Raul hopelessly.

Her last thought shocked her to her soul. She jerked upright, swinging her legs to the ground. Where had it come from? And her heart answered—last night in Raul's arms, when she'd accepted that there would never be any other man for her, only Raul.

'Penny for your thoughts, Penny?'

She jumped as Raul straddled the lounger facing hers. 'Really, Raul, not that hoary old joke.' She grimaced. Blinking, she looked across at him. He had slipped a short-sleeved shirt over his broad shoulders, but hadn't bothered to fasten the buttons or change out of his swimming trunks. She swallowed hard and mumbled, 'Is James all right?'

'Ava is busy feeding him and will then put him down for his nap; you have nothing to worry about. Relax and enjoy the sunshine, the freedom.'

'What freedom?' she mocked.

His jaw tightened and she could tell that he was curbing his anger, unusual for Raul. 'Please, Penny, can you cut out the sniping and try to listen calmly to what I have to say?' The 'please' was a surprise.

She shrugged. 'OK.'

'I know I brought you here under false pretences; perhaps I could have arranged things differently, but at the time I was furious. I have never been so enraged in my life.' He stared accusingly at her. 'You should have told me you were pregnant.'

'And you could have called me after I walked out. A simple check to make sure I got home all right wouldn't have hurt.' It still rankled Penny that Raul had not once tried to get in touch with her.

'If I had would you have told me?' Raul asked seriously.

'I don't know.'

'I did try to see you again.'

Penny's head shot up in surprise, and there was no mistaking that he was telling the truth; it was there in his eyes.

'Not straight away, I admit. We had been arguing a lot, it seemed. My pride had taken a beating and I was furious. I told myself, Let her sweat for a few weeks and then she will realise what she is missing and be my sweet, malleable Penny again.

'I went on a trip to America, and Brazil, and when I finally returned to London a month later I called at your apartment and was met by a strange man—the new owner. I asked him where the girl who used to live there was.'

Raul gave Penny a twisted smile. 'And that was when my arrogant assumption that I could have you any time bit the dust.'

'Not before time,' Penny interjected cheekily; somehow she felt a lot better knowing that Raul had at least tried to see her again.

'He told me that as far as he knew the girl had married someone called Mike from the apartment above and they were on a protracted honeymoon.'

'No!' she exclaimed. Raul could not possibly have thought she had married someone else so quickly.

'Yes,' he said, reading her mind.

'But...but,' Penny spluttered, 'it was Tanya. She shared with Amy while I was away, and then married Mike.'

'I know that. Now.' Raul said with a wry, self-mocking grin. 'But at the time I was so mad that if I had caught up with you I would have killed you.'

His confession that he had looked for her put a whole new complexion on the disastrous end of their affair. 'I never knew,' Penny said sadly, wondering what would have happened if she had stayed in London only one week longer.

'No matter.' Raul carelessly spread his hands. 'Recriminations are futile. We must concentrate on the here and now. Right?' He smiled with a kind of enquiring affection that touched her.

'Right,' she agreed, oddly subdued by Raul's revelation.

'Good,' he said. 'Progress at last. Which brings us nicely to last night when we—'

'Do we have to?' Penny cut in, the colour surging in her cheeks.

His voice sharpened. 'Yes. Last night, when you were in the throes of a nightmare, it brought home to me exactly what I had done by bringing you here against your will. I honestly had no idea you suffered that way, and I apologise. But, having said that, I do not regret the rest of the night, because I realised neither one of us has a choice.' He slanted her a heavy-lidded look. 'We both know I only have to kiss you to have you, but it works both ways. I only have to see your luscious little body and mine clenches in need—embarrassingly so sometimes.'

Penny gasped, astonished at his blunt confession.

'Don't look so surprised,' he drawled, looking oddly speculative. 'Surely you knew? You must feel what you do to me.' And, reaching across, he caught her hands in his; turning them palms up, he pressed a kiss in the centre of each hand.

A shiver, part desire and part pain, slid through her body. 'It's just sex,' she said, but knew she was lying. She loved Raul.

'Sex, lust, love—whatever name you give it, the compulsion is there between us all the time. Marriage is the logical solution for you and me and James. I have already spoken to the authorities; we can be married in three days.'

Sitting in the sun with her hands held in Raul's, Penny was tempted. It would be so easy to give in to Raul's demand. He did not love her, but she certainly loved him; she could not fool herself otherwise. Never mind that he was arrogant, overbearing and usually right. She still loved him. They could have more children . . . it was a possibility. Then out of the blue a practical problem struck her.

'Wait a minute. You told me I couldn't leave Spain because I'm technically an illegal alien. I have no passport. So how on earth could you arrange a wedding?'

His sensuous mouth tilted at the corners in a wicked smile. 'I lied. On my second visit to your apartment, while you were making coffee, I purloined your passport from the dressing-table drawer in your bedroom. James is on it, of course, so I didn't need the help of any high government official either.'

Penny's mouth fell open and she shook her head. 'You're incredible; you made me think . . .'

'An added threat to make sure you did not run away. Actually, I was surprised you believed me,' he said, stroking the palm of her hand with his thumb. 'I would never deliberately break the law. I thought you knew me better than that.'

A tingling sensation in her hand was having a disastrous effect on her brain and her ability to think clearly, but she struggled on. 'But you put James on your passport.'

'I don't consider that illegal.' His voice hardened. 'He is my son.' His dark eyes narrowed broodingly on her lovely face. 'You are procrastinating, Penny. What is it to be, yes or no?'

Life would be so easy married to Raul. 'But I have a career, a business,' she blurted out, frightened at where her thoughts were leading her.

'Ah, yes. Sense and Sensibility. I had my people look into the trading performance of the chemist. Admit it, Penny, it does not warrant two full-time pharmacists. You can easily be a silent partner and let Amy run it. In fact you would be doing her a favour.'

Why did it not surprise her that he had checked out the business? It rankled but it was typical; Raul meticulous to the nth degree. Nothing got past him. But she could not resist getting a dig in.

'As it happens, you're right. Amy and Nick plan to get married in a few months. But because of the Spanish fishermen demanding from the European Community the right to fish in English and Irish waters poor Nick's fishing boat hardly makes him a living any more.'

Raul threw back his black head and burst out laughing. 'Come on, Penny!' he finally said, grinning in genuine delight. 'You can blame me for a lot of things, but hardly for the European Community's fishing policy.'

'Yes, well . . .' Perhaps she was scraping the barrel for an excuse to deny what her head and her heart knew was really the only solution. Her lips twitched, then a chuckle escaped. She looked into his dark eyes, saw the amusement and laughed with him. 'Perhaps I did go a bit too far.'

Raul stood up and hauled her with him. A flash of pleasure caught her unawares as his naked thighs brushed hers, and she stopped laughing and looked up at him.

'Will you go that little bit further and agree to marry me?' he asked quietly. His strong hands moved and framed her face, and made her look at him. 'Be reasonable, for James's sake.'

'I don't know,' she said slowly. 'You did kidnap the pair of us. Hardly the action of a reasonable man.'

'I was frightened,' Raul said soberly.

'You, frightened?' she exclaimed; the concept was unbelievable. Privately Penny thought that in a past life Raul could have been a swashbuckling pirate, like Errol Flynn in the old black and white movies she had a secret penchant for watching.

'I am human, Penny; I do have the same hopes and fears as other men. The day I heard your name on the television—Penelope Gold—and realised that you were not married and the next second that I had a son, I was shocked rigid. Then a moment later to discover the child had been stolen was the most terrifying experience of my life. When I met you and James I was furious at your deceit, and frustrated at my inability to do anything to protect you both, but I did not dare upset you.'

'I never thought,' Penny murmured, and she should have done. When they had first been lovers he had insisted on taking her virtually everywhere with him. He was a possessive and protective male. Even when he had sent her back from Dubai it had been for her own protection. He'd considered that she would be safer in Spain.

But what did he mean, he hadn't dared upset her? It sure as hell had upset her to find herself kidnapped, she thought with a flash of resentment. And as soon as the question entered her head she was asking the question. 'What do you mean, upset me?'

'You were in shock and wearing yourself out, still working and trying to pretend everything was normal while never letting the boy out of your sight. I could not allow it to continue. I spoke to your doctor and he agreed with me—you needed to rest, a chance to recuperate from a devastatingly emotional experience. But if I had suggested you come to Spain for a holiday you would have laughed in my face. Therefore I took the decision for you.'

Penny frowned, pulling away for a moment. *Had* she been living on the edge for the past few weeks? she asked herself, and the answer was yes, the frequent nightmares proved it. 'You're so convinced you have the answer to everything,' she said in a soft, pain-filled voice. 'You frighten me sometimes.'

He looked down at her and grimaced. 'I don't mean to. And if I had not given the wrong answer years ago none of this would have happened. But it is not too late.' And before she could guess his intention his dark head lowered and he pressed his mouth against her parted lips. 'James deserves two parents, and we are good together,' he whispered into her mouth, and then proceeded to show her.

By the time Raul allowed her to breathe again she was in no state to deny him anything.

'Have you made up your mind, Penny?'

'Yes,' she said softly. 'All right.'

His dark eyes gleamed with golden shards of triumph and a latent passion. 'You won't regret it, I promise, and I will not be too demanding a husband; in fact the marriage need not be for life, simply until James is of age. Then you can resume your career—anything you like.'

If he thought that he was reassuring her he was wrong. 'That's very reasonable of you,' she said flatly, pushing out of his arms. His words hurt, leaving her in no doubt. It was James that he wanted, and she was simply tolerated as his mother and a compatible sexual partner. But she had committed herself now. God help her!

CHAPTER TEN

'BUT it is ridiculous, Raul.' It was four o'clock in the afternoon on the eve of their wedding. James was playing quite happily in a plastic sandpit that had appeared the day before at Raul's instructions, and Penny, wearing a brief green bikini—a relic from the past—had been sitting on a nearby lounger, supervising her son. Now she was standing, hands on hips, glaring up at her soon-to-be husband.

Raul, wearing hip-hugging jeans and a short-sleeved white shirt with a buttoned-down collar left open to reveal the beginnings of black chest hair, looked dangerously sexy and very sure of himself. 'It's tradition, Penny.' He grinned down at her. 'You know that.'

She felt herself shiver, intensely aware of him though he wasn't even touching her. 'But there is no point in your stopping at a hotel for the night. We have been sharing the same bed for the past couple of nights; we already have a child, for heaven's sake!'

Not for a moment dared she admit even to herself that she was frightened—frightened of being on her own, with time to think. As long as Raul was around she had swanned along in a kind of mental daze.

He had reintroduced her to Daisy, her horse, as well as providing the tiniest Shetland pony that Penny had ever seen for James. They had spent the long, lazy days with James and the passionate nights locked in each other's arms. When she'd had any doubts about the forthcoming marriage Raul, with unerring accuracy, had seemed to sense her feelings and, before she had been able to voice them, had either physically or mentally reassured her.

Yesterday he had arranged for the owner of an exclusive boutique in Granada to visit the *hacienda* with a choice of designer clothes. Then Raul had done the traditional thing and disappeared while Penny had chosen a fabulous heavy wild silk dress for the wedding. Now he was adamant that he was spending the wedding eve at a hotel in Granada.

Given the circumstances, she should be flattered that he was leaving her alone, she conceded grudgingly. He obviously trusted her enough not to renege on her promise to marry him and disappear. But she still could not resist saying huskily, 'Must you?'

'It's bad luck, Penny, and we need all the luck we can get.' His mouth twisted into a mockery of a smile. 'You of all people must recognise that.'

The edge of bitterness in his tone stopped her short. He obviously had still not forgiven or forgotten that she had kept his son from her.

'Papa, Papa. Castle.' James's voice split the tense silence between the two adults.

They both looked to where James was sitting in the sand and smiled. The little boy had sand in his hair and all over his body, but he was beaming triumphantly, having finally succeeded in heaping up a mound of sand almost as high as his chest.

'He makes it all worthwhile,' Raul said quietly, and, glancing down at Penny, planted a brief kiss on the top of her head. 'See you tomorrow at the church. Carlos will drive you. Be good.'

He strolled over to James, lifted the little boy up, congratulated him on his great castle, kissed him, then lowered him back in the sandpit. 'You too, little one,' he murmured, and, turning, he walked across to where his car waited, a suitcase already in the boot.

Penny watched him drive away with a dull ache in her heart. She knew that he did not love her, but knowing that he had looked for her over two years ago had given her hope; and now, to be reminded that they were marrying for the child was a blow to her self-confidence.

She knew that she could satisfy Raul on a purely physical level, and her secret hope was that in time he would learn to love her. But sometimes she could not help wondering if she was fooling herself...

An hour later she knew she was...

Busily drying James with a large, fluffy towel after their last dip in the pool for the day, and singing 'Four and Twenty Blackbirds' at the same time, Penny didn't hear the sleek sports car pull up in front of the house. It was only when James shouted, 'Lady. Lady, Mamma,' that Penny realised they were not alone.

She knew it could not be Ava, as Ava and Carlos had left earlier for some last-minute shopping. Setting James down on his feet, she pulled a sweatshirt over his head and turned with interest to greet the unexpected visitor.

Small, black-haired, and wearing a figure-hugging yellow skirt with matching short jacket, black eyes glinting maliciously—there was no mistaking the woman. Penny's heart pounded erratically, colour surging in her face. She winced at her own stupidity. 'Dulcie.' She said the name under her breath. How could she have forgotten?

'*Buenos días*, Penny. So this is the child that has caused all the uproar and scandal. I simply had to see for myself,' Dulcie drawled in her native Spanish.

Penny responded in kind. '*Buenos días*. And what scandal is that?' she asked flatly, her eyes clashing with

Dulcie's dark, venomous gaze, then dropping to the other woman's hand. Her heart froze in her chest. Dulcie wore the huge diamond engagement ring that Penny had first seen in the magazine photograph on the fatal day when James had been abducted.

'Why, the fact that Raul Da Silva, one of the most influential and revered men in the area, would ignore his obligations and dishonour his family name by lowering himself to marry someone like you simply because of a child that may or may not be his.'

She heard the words as if from a long way off, numb with shock. 'Obligations' could only mean one thing. Raul and Dulcie were or had been engaged. All the colour drained from Penny's face; she felt as if someone had twisted a knife in her stomach and gutted her. Involuntarily she picked James up in her arms, cuddling him to her icy body.

'James is Raul's son—' she stared bleakly at Dulcie '—whatever you may think.' But she could not deny the rest of Dulcie's malicious statement. She suddenly realised that she had been floating along in a sensual daze, accepting Raul's proposal, pretending to herself that it was a rational decision, when all the time she had been avoiding reality.

'I've got to hand it to you, Penny; you're cleverer than I thought. At least the child has Raul's colouring—and the poor man is desperate for an heir.'

Penny bent her head to disguise the anguish in her eyes. But she could make no response, because she knew that Dulcie was right.

'Of course, you know that if I could have children Raul and I would have been married when you two split up, but under the circumstances there did not seem to be any need to rush.'

Penny slowly raised her head. James squirmed to be put down and gently she set him on his feet, keeping a tight grip on his little hand, more for her own support than his. She stood up. Her legs trembled but she stared Dulcie straight in the face and gave a bitter, forced smile. 'Then I have to thank you for my good luck and your bad fortune,' she managed to say sarcastically, amazed that her voice did not crack in the process.

Dulcie's eyes leapt with anger and something almost maniacal. 'Don't fool yourself that he loves you. Raul will always come back to me. He always has.' And with that vicious parting shot Dulcie turned on her heel and strode across the courtyard to her car, leaving Penny frozen to the spot, still grasping James but feeling unutterably alone. She wanted to cry, but instead James broke the silence.

'Not nice lady, Mamma.'

Out of the mouths of babes! she thought sadly. And, gritting her teeth, she lifted James up in her arms and walked into the house, appalled at her own gullibility. Raul had never cared for her. He never would. She had been kidding herself to think for a second that she could win his love. He had given it years ago to the woman who had just left.

Entering the kitchen, she acted on autopilot, preparing James's supper while he sat happily on the floor playing with a soup ladle and a couple of stainless-steel pans. For once she was grateful for the racket he made. It stopped her from having to think.

Ava arrived back from the town with Carlos, all smiles; she had found the perfect hat for the wedding.

Penny admired the hat and said all the right things, but her heart wasn't in it. It was slowly breaking into a million pieces.

She had no idea afterwards how she got through the next few hours. She bathed and bedded James down for the night. She changed into jeans and black sweater, then sat in the kitchen and pushed the dinner Ava had prepared around on her plate. And, when the telephone rang, and Ava answered it and Penny heard the name 'Raul', she got to her feet and dashed out.

'Wait,' Ava called after her. 'It is for you. Señor Raul.'

She could not trust herself to speak to him. 'Tell him it's bad luck.' She furiously threw his own words back at a shocked Ava as she ran upstairs and into the master bedroom.

She stopped, her glance skimming over the wide bed, and she shuddered, closing her eyes against the tears that threatened to overwhelm her fragile self-control. Maturity had taught her nothing. She clenched her small hands into fists, her nails digging into her palms till she broke the skin, but she did not feel the physical pain. The mental anguish was tearing her apart.

She stifled a moan from the depths of her being. Raul, with an ease that betrayed her naïvety, had got her back into his bed and under his spell with hardly a whimper from her. Slowly she opened her eyes, her face set and pale. Deliberately she turned, closed the door and locked it. Never again, she vowed silently. Never again...

She was leaving with James; even if she had to drug the security guards and walk to the nearest town she didn't care. Not any more. She knew that she had only herself to blame in a way. She had forgotten Dulcie—or perhaps her mind had simply blocked out the other woman, in much the same way that she had refused to think about the abduction of James once she'd had him back. Perhaps it was the mind's way of protecting one from a pain too fierce to bear, she thought. But, God help her, she was hurting now!

Gritting her teeth, she found a suitcase in the back of the wardrobe and haphazardly threw a few clothes in it. Her head spun; she needed her passport. It was probably in Raul's study. A bitter smile distorted her full lips at the memory of another one of his lies.

Manhandling the open suitcase onto the wide bed, she sat down beside it to catch her breath. All she needed now was to pack James enough clothes to last for a few days and they were ready. But was she?

Where was she going? she asked herself desperately. Back to Cornwall? Even if they made it, Raul would not be far behind them, and did she really want to go back to Cornwall? She stared with sightless eyes at the wall opposite, a pale, tragic facsimile of the girl she had once been.

Slowly, as she relived the past in her mind, she recognised a painful truth. She was not the strong, decisive person she had thought herself to be. Instead she had spent most of her life simply reacting to the circumstances around her.

As a teenager she'd assumed that she would study medicine in memory of her father, not because she'd had any great desire to be a doctor. When she'd failed to get the marks required, and after the death of her mother, she had not picked a career in pharmacy. It had picked her, simply because the company she'd worked for Saturdays as a schoolgirl had offered to sponsor her through pharmaceutical college.

Her affair with Raul had followed the same pattern. He'd made love to her and asked her to move in with him. Deep down she had wanted marriage, but she'd allowed herself to settle for less. She had been doing it all her life. Easygoing Penny. She never made a fuss.

If she was honest the idea for Sense and Sensibility had been more Amy's than hers. The way they had found the shop—driving through Cornwall to a wedding and passing through Royal Harton. If they had checked thoroughly before buying the place they would easily have discovered that the plans had been passed for a new health centre with a pharmacy some twenty miles away. But they hadn't.

Once, just once, she had made a firm stand and asked Raul to marry her, and look where that got her. Total rejection...

She'd even got pregnant by accident—not that she regretted it for a second. Penny drew a shaky breath. And her biggest mistake of all—she had carelessly handed over her child to the first nurse who'd asked, and in consequence Raul had stormed back into her life.

She cringed with shame and humiliation. God, but she was some kind of prize idiot! Did she have 'Pushover' carved on her brow? she wondered bitterly.

Then the final fiasco—she'd let both James and herself be abducted by Raul. She'd fallen into his arms, and his bed, with hardly a murmur, then meekly agreed to marry him because she loved him, even though she knew he did not love her. Once again the line of least resistance...

Penny shivered, a draught of evening air wafting through the open window. She glanced at the swaying curtains and noted that it was dark outside. She had no notion of how long she had sat mulling over the past, but she guessed it was late.

Jumping to her feet, she swore under her breath. But not too late! She straightened her shoulders, a new stiffness in her spine, her decision made.

She switched on the bedside light and crossed to the dressing table. She glanced at her reflection—the wide, haunted eyes and the soft, tremulous mouth—and despised what she saw.

She clenched her teeth, her lips firming in a tight, narrow line. She was taking charge of her own life. She was finished with going with the flow. She was going to start making her own waves, and the first one would wash right over Raul Da Silva and get him out of her life for good. She wasn't running away. She was going downstairs to call him and tell him that the wedding was off...

A knock at the door brought her head round. 'Yes,' she said, firmly expecting it to be Ava. She saw the handle turn.

'Open the door, Penny.'

She flinched, surprised at the sound of Raul's voice, but the bitter knowledge of Raul's callous manipulation of her—and, she recognised, the unfortunate Dulcie—was eating into her soul. A steely determination to stand up for herself had her marching across the room and unlocking the door.

Raul brushed past her. His dark eyes flicked around the room and noted the suitcase. Slowly he turned to where Penny stood with her back to the door. 'I thought we decided no honeymoon just yet. Too much upset for James.' His dark eyes were hooded, masking his expression. 'Or have I got it wrong?' he drawled cynically.

It took a great effort to meet and hold his gaze, but she did. 'You've got it wrong,' she said steadily.

His eyes narrowed, and she sensed the fury lying beneath the surface of his control. 'Are you going to make me drag it out of you? Why the suitcase?' he demanded hardly.

Penny swallowed nervously, not feeling quite so brave. 'Because I'm leaving you.'

'I knew it.' His dark eyes flashed murderously. 'I bloody knew it,' he swore, and lunged forward, grasping her upper arms in a vice-like grip. 'You are not leaving.

You are not going anywhere,' he snarled, hurting her, his cool control cracked wide open. 'I will not allow it.'

He dragged her towards him and she got a whiff of strong alcohol on his breath. She was so surprised that she forgot to be afraid and really looked at him. This was a Raul she had never seen before; his hair was dishevelled and he needed a shave.

'You've been drinking.' Raul never drank—well, only in moderation. Then she noticed that he was wearing the same clothes as he had been in when he'd left hours ago. She knew the hotel he was staying at had a strict dress code and stupidly asked, 'Have you had dinner?'

'You're walking out on me and you ask have I had dinner? Have I been drinking? Are you mad?' Raul exclaimed harshly. 'Yes, I've been damned well drinking; I've been pacing the hotel room, telling myself I was doing the noble thing, that I could trust you. Until I could stand it no longer and rang you.'

Then he pushed her towards the bed; she felt the edge of the mattress at the back of her knees just before he thrust her down, knocking the suitcase to the floor as he did so.

He hovered over her, his hands on her shoulders, forcing her to sit on the bed. She bent her head, unable to face the fury in his eyes. 'I did not want to speak to you,' she said, gulping down her fear.

'I gathered that from Ava. Why else would I break the law and drive after sinking three brandies?' he snarled. 'Only you could make me so careless.'

'You had no need to drive back tonight on my account,' she shot back, and looked defiantly up into his hard face. She glimpsed the brief flare of terrible rage as his eyes burned into hers, threatening her very soul. She licked her tongue over parched lips and forced herself to continue. 'It changes nothing. James and I are leaving in the morning.' And, drawing on every ounce of courage she possessed, she added, 'There will be no wedding.'

For a long moment Raul looked capable of murder, his face rigid with fury. The taut silence was deafening as his fingers dug into her shoulders like the claws of some wild cat. Penny drew in a sharp breath, fighting down pain and panic. Then his eyes hardened until they resembled black jet, his mouth curved in a chilling smile.

'Oh, yes, there will,' he drawled implacably. 'I refuse to be deserted twice in one lifetime.'

He pushed her, and she fell backwards on the bed. Raul followed her down, his lips capturing hers in a cruel, punishing kiss. His mouth forced hers apart, plundering and possessing in savage domination. She struggled, trying to get away, her clenched fists pounding his broad back in bitter rage and frustration at her own inability to escape. But, bent over the edge of the bed, with his powerfully muscled thighs straddling hers, it was no contest.

Altering her tactics, with one almighty effort she punched him in the chest and tore her mouth away from his.

'That is all you think about,' she screamed up into his face. 'Your stupid pride. Well, you have nothing to worry about,' she told him furiously. 'Dulcie will quite happily oblige tomorrow; she told me so herself, and she was wearing your ring to prove it. You don't need me. You never did, you lying, cheating two-timing bastard.'

Her chest heaved; she was panting for breath, but she was glad that she had finally told Raul exactly what she thought of him.

Her blue eyes spitting fire, she watched him, expecting a violent explosion any second. To her amazement it never happened. Bracing himself on his hands either side of her body, he glanced down at her flushed, furious face then closed his eyes. The silence stretched until it was an almost tangible thing. She was damned if she was going to be the first to break it; even so she regarded him with a certain wariness, conscious of the hard weight of his thighs holding her hostage.

Raul opened his eyes, and there was no mistaking the sorrow and regret in their black depths. 'But I do need you, Penny,' he said in a raw voice. 'Dulcie could never in a million years be a substitute for you.'

He might look contrite, but Penny did not believe it for a minute. 'Only because she can't have children,' she snapped back.

Raul's broad forehead creased in a frown, and she glimpsed a curiously speculative gleam in his dark eyes. Then she saw a muscle jerk wildly under the dark skin of his jaw and his face go rigid. 'That bloody woman,' he burst out. 'I might have guessed.' And he cursed long and fluently in Spanish before saying grittily, 'She was here today, wasn't she?'

'Y-e-s,' Penny answered slowly, not sure why he was asking.

'What did she say?' he demanded, and when she did not answer immediately Raul lowered his dark head to within inches of her face. 'Tell me, Penny,' he drawled, 'or I'll have to make you.'

With Raul still straddling her, she was suddenly not so much angry as very aware of the danger of the situation.

'Oh, I was treated to her usual vilification. I was the lowest of the low, and by marrying me you were dishonouring your name, welching on your obligations. I can't say I blame the woman. It must be hard to find your fiancé is marrying someone else. But then you would know all about that,' she drawled sarcastically. 'You and her seem to be about even on that score.'

She saw his dark eyes widen in shock, and then he rolled off her to sit up on the edge of the bed, his head in his hands. Penny dragged herself up to a sitting position and, shooting him a sidelong glance, added jeeringly, 'Truth hurt, does it?'

Raul lifted his head, his dark eyes seeking hers. 'You have it all wrong, Penny, and it is all my fault,' he declared harshly, and, reaching across her body, he brushed the hair back from her face with an unsteady hand, the better to see her expression. 'First, I am not engaged to Dulcie.' His hand stopped at the side of her neck, forcing her to face him. 'I have no interest in the woman whatsoever,' he declared adamantly. 'It was all over seventeen years ago. She was a boyish mistake, and I was eternally grateful when she married someone else.'

'Hah!' Penny snorted. 'You've got a funny way of showing "no interest"—giving the woman a ring, posing for a photograph in a glossy magazine. You're too damn right, it's all your fault.'

All her resentment and bitterness spilled out; she knew she was being unfair but once she had started she could not stop. 'I saw the picture of the pair of you while James and I waited for the doctor. If I hadn't got such a shock maybe I would have had the sense not to hand over my child to the bogus nurse.' She was unaware of what she was revealing by her outburst.

'Oh, my God!'

She did not see the horror in his gaze, and even if she had she was too mad to care. 'You and that woman cost me a day of my child's life and you expect me to believe she is nothing to you? Don't make me laugh,' she mocked. 'I seem to remember, the last time I was here, that you were adamant I had to apologise to the woman. And we were supposed to be partners at the time . . . such loyalty I can do without.' Penny was not listening to his excuses; she had had enough to last a lifetime.

'I had no idea you felt like that! Believed that!' Raul said fiercely. 'You're wrong, so wrong.' And his free hand caught her shoulders, curving her into his side. She stiffened and tried to pull away, but he was bigger and much stronger and easily crushed her against him. '*Dios*, I have a lot to apologise for, Penny,' he groaned. 'But I can't let you go.'

She tipped back her chin and glanced defiantly up at him, about to argue. But she was struck dumb as, for a second, she saw his heart in his eyes, the rigid mask of self-control vanquished by a naked vulnerability she had never seen before.

'Because I love you,' he rasped.

Her blue eyes were like saucers. Her heart jumped violently and her mouth fell open in shock.

'I know I can't expect you to love me after the way I have behaved, but I still want you to marry me tomorrow as we planned.' He stared fixedly at her. 'But you don't have to. I realise now I can't force you. But please let me explain before you decide. Surely you can give me that much?'

If he really loved her, she would give him anything. Penny trembled at the thought, but still could not quite believe his avowal of love. 'Explain,' she said shakily.

His arm eased a little around her shoulders and his hand at her neck slid around to cup her chin. His brown eyes burned with some fierce emotion. 'It might take some time. I have made so many mistakes I hardly know where to start,' he said hesitantly, and his hesitation gave her hope. It was so unlike the Raul she knew.

'From the moment I met you, Penny, I knew you were going to be very special to me. I loved your happy, carefree smile, your wholehearted enjoyment of life, and

I vowed to have you for myself. After the first night we spent together I should have married you. God knows, I loved you.'

The hope burnt higher in Penny's heart. 'You never said,' she had to remind him.

'I was frightened. One woman had already virtually stood me up at the altar. Not that it bothered me much. But the fact that you were so much younger than me did... My father married a woman years younger than himself and it didn't work. My mother ran off with a man her own age. It was cowardly of me, I know, and I'm not trying to make excuses, but we are all shaped in some way by our past.'

Ava had been right, Penny thought wonderingly, staring at him, her heart thumping faster in her breast. Perhaps he was telling her the truth...

'And, being brutally honest, once you moved in with me I was as happy as a bull in clover.'

'I seem to remember you acted like one,' Penny said reminiscently, with the beginnings of a smile tilting her full lips.

He gave her a wry grin in return. 'I know. I can't seem to help myself around you. That was part of my problem.'

'Sex?' she said, puzzled; that was the only part of their relationship where there was no problem, she thought.

'Sex, love and all that goes with it. In my case, total possessiveness and insane jealousy. The night in Dubai when I fought with you about the Arab it was pure jealousy. I didn't like the way I acted. I surprised myself. I shipped you back to Spain and then found you had left the bracelet I had given you.'

His confession of jealousy was music to Penny's ears, but she was still wary of this oddly humble Raul. One delicate brow arched sardonically. 'Hardly surprising, he speed you rushed me out of the hotel.'

'Have you ever worn it? Have you still got it?' Raul queried, his eyes avoiding hers.

'I don't wear it.' She could not admit that after they'd parted she had not been able to bear to look at it. 'It's in a safe-deposit box at the bank. I thought I would keep it for James's college fund,' she explained, but wondered why he was going on about it.

Then his gaze flicked back to hers. 'Did you ever read the inscription on the back of the clasp?'

'Inscription? What inscription?'

'*Dios*, what a fool I have been.' And, sweeping her into his arms, he hugged her tightly, burying his face in her soft, scented hair.

'Raul,' she murmured against his chest, and placed a hand on his arm, pushing him back slightly. She glanced up, puzzled. And he smiled—a smile of pure joy.

'Don't you see, Penny, our troubles started when I joined you again here at the *hacienda*? I was furious because you had left the bracelet in the hotel in Dubai. Remember I asked you if you had missed anything else besides me and you said no?'

She remembered the conversation, but had never linked it with the bracelet. 'Yes, but—'

Raul cut in. 'Engraved on the clasp is "Raul loves Penny"—a simple message but it's true. When you never missed it or mentioned it I got it into my head that you didn't care very much. Señor Costas told me you had ordered his daughter from the house—for no good reason, according to Dulcie—and I was angry. In my own defence I must point out I had no idea Dulcie was such a bitch.'

'I...' She stopped, choked with emotion as the enormity of Raul's revelation sank into her head and

heart. He had to be telling the truth, because she stil
had the bracelet and could prove it. Her blue eyes mist
with tears, she wondered sadly how it had all gone s
wrong, and knew that she must share some of the blame

'I did try to tell you,' Penny said softly. 'But at th
time you had sent me back to Spain so suddenly that
was feeling pretty resentful myself. I was rude, I admit
But when you sent me on my own again to London tha
really hurt. I was beginning to feel like some unwante
baggage.'

Raul cuddled her closer. 'Never unwanted, Penny. Bu
I should have believed you and trusted you. It was shee
bloody-mindedness on my part. I was afraid of th
depths of my feelings for you, and of losing you. Th
day after you left for England Ava lashed into me an
I learnt the truth.

'I tackled Dulcie about it and she was full of apologie
and insisted it was the trauma of her broken marriag
that had made her behave so badly. I didn't believe he
but neither did I care enough about the woman to b
bothered. But you I cared quite desperately about. An
when I called you that night and you were out all nigh
my fear of losing you turned to pure fury. But it did n
stop me dashing to London to find you.'

'I was lying on the sofa and you woke me up; yo
were so cold.' Penny shivered at the memory.

Raul, feeling her shiver, lifted her onto his lap. 'Better
he murmured; his dark eyes, shadowed with remorse
fused with Penny's. 'I will never forgive myself as lon
as I live for what I did that day. It must have taken
lot of nerve to propose to me. I wanted to say yes an
carry you off to the church. But my stubborn pride an
a grim determination not to be manipulated by an
woman stopped me—plus the bracelet burning a hole i

my pocket yet again. Can you ever forgive me and try to love me?'

He was a stubborn, proud, rather conservative macho male, but he was also the only man she would ever love... And she finally believed him. A surge of euphoric relief shuddered through her.

'I forgive you.' She smiled into his serious eyes. But she wasn't quite ready to declare that she loved him; there were a few unanswered questions, and she didn't want anything to stand in the way of their future happiness. 'And I might do more,' she drawled softly, and linked her arms around his neck, 'if you can explain how you ended up in a magazine with Dulcie on your arm.'

'Is that jealousy I hear?' Raul teased, but, looking into her eyes, he saw the lingering doubt and continued in a more serious vein. 'It was a charity evening in aid of cancer research at a Madrid theatre. The elderly widower Dulcie is engaged to was the guest speaker. He left her with me while he went on stage to deliver his speech—'

'Dulcie is engaged to someone else?' Penny interjected.

'Yes, and you should not be too hard on her, Penny; it is a terrible thing for a woman not to be able to have children. I think that is why Dulcie is the way she is.'

'You're right,' Penny said softly, thinking of the joy her own son gave her. 'But it still does not explain the photograph,' she tacked on.

'It was a celebrity affair, Penny; they took hundreds of photographs. It surprised me that they bothered to include Dulcie and me, when there were so many film stars and the like around. But I promise you I delivered Dulcie back to her fiancé, pledged a donation and left. Alone.'

Cuddled on Raul's lap, the solid comfort of his arms around her, she looked deep into his compelling eyes and knew that he was telling the truth.

'I have been alone from the moment you left me,' Raul admitted, his deep voice husky with emotion as his gaze roamed over her face only inches from his own. 'When I thought you were married to someone else I almost lost my mind. Ask Ava if you don't believe me. I made her life hell.

'I drank too much, until Ava stole my car keys and hid all the liquor in the house. We had a stand-up row, and when I caught myself lifting my hand to her the full horror of what I had become hit me.'

'Oh, Raul.' She was shaken by the bleakness in his tone, and inexplicably she wanted to reassure him. 'You might look and act like a medieval pirate on the Spanish Main sometimes—' her lips twitched in the briefest of smiles '—but you would never hit a woman. I know that much for sure.'

'Thank you, I think,' he said wryly, and brushed his lips across hers in the lightest of caresses before continuing. 'I threw myself into my work in the faint hope that I might be able to catch a couple of hours' sleep at night without suffering the torment of the damned, thinking of you and how we were together. There has been no other woman in my life since you left me, Penny. If I can't have you, I don't want anyone.'

His strong hand moved caressingly up and down her back. Penny stayed silent, realising that they had both suffered over the past couple of years.

'I will die a bitter, celibate old man without you.'

'You, celibate?' she cried, her eyes widening in shock. Raul had always been a powerfully sensual man, with an overwhelming masculine virility he had never attempted to hide—that much she remembered clearly from their affair. 'Bitter, maybe—celibate, never,' she opined bluntly.

'You don't understand,' he growled with an edge of frustration. 'Nothing matters—work, the ranch; without you my life is meaningless. You are my life force, Penny,' he told her huskily, his mouth grazing hers again.

Her lips parted to respond, but the raw intensity in his eyes made her catch her breath. Then he kissed her brow, her eyes, the curve of her cheek.

'Surely you must know, must sense how I feel?' he whispered urgently against her ear, his hot breath causing her pulse to leap into overdrive. 'When I'm with you, intimately joined to you . . .' he groaned, his hard thighs moving restlessly beneath her bottom, making her aware of his aroused state. 'When I move in you, feel you clench around me, I know how paradise feels. I know the meaning of life. I feel as though we are one with the universe—an exquisite perfect whole that no one can destroy.'

And, slowly twisting, he laid her down on the bed, his long body half covering hers, and he kissed her hard on the mouth—a long, slow kiss full of unspoken promise that made her tremble in his arms . . .

'I love you desperately, obsessively, in every way there is,' Raul declared huskily. 'You have to believe me.'

Penny, her vision blurring with tears of joy, threaded her fingers through his black hair and held his beloved face firmly in her small hands. 'I do believe you, and I do love you, Raul. There has never been anyone else for me. Only you.'

He stared at her, the pupils of his dark eyes dilating with passion. 'You—'

She pressed her mouth to his, swallowing his words, putting her heart and soul into the kiss. Raul's arms encircled her, his weight crushing her, but she didn't care.

She was where she wanted to be, locked in her lover's arms and at last free to declare her love with no fear of rejection.

Raul raised his head and took a deep, shuddering breath as he stared down at her. 'Lord, tell me I'm not dreaming.'

Penny playfully tugged his ear and he yelped. 'You're not dreaming.' She grinned.

But Raul did not return her smile. 'And will you marry me, Penny, be my wife, my love?' he asked bluntly. 'No more doubt, no more running away. I couldn't stand to lose you a second time.'

'You aren't asking me to marry you simply to get James? Dulcie hinted as much,' Penny voiced her last secret fear.

'Damn Dulcie! I love James, and I want to be a good father to him and—God willing—watch him grow into a fine man. But you I love more than life; without you everything else will lose its lustre. Marry me. Please...' The wealth of feeling in his impassioned plea convinced Penny.

'Yes, Raul.'

The soft avowal was all it took. In minutes they were both naked, Penny's hands clenched on his shoulders, her head threshing from side to side, her eyes closed in ecstasy as Raul kissed every inch of her body with a burning intensity, worshipping her feminine form, parting her thighs, his caresses unbelievably intimate.

'You're so sexy, so hot,' he growled against her stomach. Then, rearing up, he lifted her to accept his pulsing manhood. 'You do want me,' he shouted hoarsely. 'You do.'

She felt the pleasure, the excitement pounding through her body, and did not begrudge him his thoroughly masculine growl of triumph.

*   *   *

A long time later Penny stirred in his arms. She leaned up and smiled down at his sleeping face. She flicked his bottom lip with her finger. 'Raul...'

'What?' he queried, half-asleep.

'I think you'd better leave now.'

'What?' he queried, half-asleep.

'I think you'd better leave now.'

'What?' he shouted. His eyes flying wide open, he hauled her down on top of him. 'You're crazy, woman.' He nuzzled her neck.

'But what about tradition?' Penny teased.

'To hell with tradition,' Raul said pithily. 'From now on I am going to be one of these New Men I hear so much about. Equal partners—sharing the load, sharing the bed.'

Penny burst out laughing, levered herself away from him and rolled on her back, still laughing. 'Sharing the bed is about the only part you would get right,' she chortled.

'So it's a start,' Raul drawled, and, looping an arm around her, cradled her tight to his side. 'The rest you can teach me.' And he kissed the top of her head and yawned.

Grinning, Penny cuddled up against him. Raul a New Man? Never. He was far too arrogantly male.

And then she paused for thought. But he was a thinking and caring man—she remembered him describing his work and his hopes for the new low-cost desalination plants. And he was sensitive to both her and their son's needs. He had admitted that he'd been afraid to upset her when they'd first met again. Maybe he was not such a hopeless case after all, she mused happily as she fell asleep.

*   *   *

She was convinced the next day when she stepped out
of the bridal car at the entrance to the church of San
Marcos in the tiny village on the boundary of Raul's
estate.

The ivory wild silk dress, with its high ruffled neck
and fitted bodice, accentuated her tiny waist, and the
skirt, a multitude of fine pleats, floated around her legs
as she walked; the effect was Victorian and demure, yet
stunning. She nervously clutched Carlos's arm as they
entered the church, and then a scream of delight escaped
her.

Waiting in the porch was James, dressed in a cute blue
velvet suit, but beside him stood Amy, her face glowing
almost as much as her ginger hair, and dressed in a gown
complementary to Penny's.

'I don't believe it!' Penny cried.

'Would I miss your wedding?' Amy grinned. 'Anyway,
your husband-to-be insisted, and he's a hard man to
deny. Nick even agreed to be best man—though he'd
sworn never to set foot in Spain after the fishing debacle.'

The two girls laughed and hugged until Amy drew back
and said, 'Time to go, friend. Be happy.'

Penny stepped into the church, her gaze flying straight
to the proud head and broad back of Raul, standing at
the altar. Her almost New Man, she thought, his con-
sideration flooding her already full heart as she slowly
began to the walk down the aisle on Carlos's arm.

Raul turned; his dark eyes, full of love, caught and
held hers. Then, as though he could not help himself,
he walked towards her, relieved Carlos of his duties and
possessively pulled her slender arm through his and
walked her the rest of the way to the altar himself.

Amy laughed, the congregation laughed, and even the priest had trouble hiding his chuckle as he read the marriage service.

But Penny and Raul didn't care. They were in a world of their own as they vowed their undying love and sealed it with a kiss . . .

FREE

Return this coupon and we'll send you 4 Mills & Boon® romance novels and a mystery gift absolutely FREE! We'll even pay the postage and packing for you.

We're making you this offer to introduce you to the benefits of Reader Service: FREE home delivery of brand-new Mills & Boon romance novels, at least a month before they are available in the shops, FREE gifts and a monthly Newsletter packed with information.

Accepting these FREE books and gift places you under no obligation to buy, you may cancel at any time, even after receiving just your free shipment. Simply complete the coupon below and send it to:

MILLS & BOON READER SERVICE, FREEPOST, CROYDON, SURREY, CR9 3WZ.

No stamp needed

Yes, please send me 4 free Mills & Boon Romance novels and a mystery gift. I understand that unless you hear from me, I will receive 6 superb new titles every month for just £2.10* each postage and packing free. I am under no obligation to purchase any books and I may cancel or suspend my subscription at any time, but the free books and gifts will be mine to keep in any case. (I am over 18 years of age)

2EP6R

Ms/Mrs/Miss/Mr _____

Address _____

_____

_____ Postcode _____

mps
MAILING
PREFERENCE
SERVICE

MILLS & BOON®

Next Month's Romances

Each month you can choose from a wide variety of romance with Mills & Boon®. Below are the new titles to look out for next month.

THE TROPHY HUSBAND	Lynne Graham
RENDEZVOUS WITH REVENGE	Miranda Lee
RUNNING WILD	Alison Fraser
MARRIAGE BY ARRANGEMENT	Sally Wentworth
A PROPER WIFE	Sandra Marton
INTIMATE RELATIONS	Elizabeth Oldfield
MOVING IN WITH ADAM	Jeanne Allan
GROUNDS FOR MARRIAGE	Daphne Clair
AMBER'S WEDDING	Sara Wood
HAVING IT ALL!	Emma Richmond
THE PERFECT MALE	Rosemary Hammond
FOR BABY'S SAKE	Val Daniels
ENTICED	Jennifer Taylor
VIRGIN TERRITORY	Suzanne Carey
AT FIRST SIGHT	Eva Rutland
COUNTERFEIT COWGIRL	Heather Allison